# Snow Hill

## By Joseph McGee

BLU PHI'ER PUBLISHING, L.L.C.
MARSHALL, TEXAS
WWW.BLUPHIER.COM

Library of Congress Control Number: 2008933024

ISBN: 978-0-9799884-8-6

Printed in the U.S.A.
First Edition July 2008

# Acknowledgements

I always feel compelled to write a long, overdrawn acknowledgement section that seems dreadfully boring to those poor souls who'll read this book. But to those whose names I mention below, I hope this will mean something to them.

First, I have to thank Eric Enck who gave this novel the push in the right direction and put it on top of the ever-growing slush pile of the publisher.

I owe thanks to Leya Booth who had helped significantly with the editing of this book to make it as good as it is. (Genius Office Services, for those aspiring writers out there — she's the best at what she does!)

Joe McKinney for his friendship and kind words. And I didn't even need to pay him to write a kind little something about *In the Wake of the Night* on Amazon.com — honest!

Lara Dean, editor of *The Pulse Magazine* in my hometown of Worcester. She gave me the chance for my first local interview back in October of 2006, and accepted some freelance material, which leads me to say a quick thanks to Christopher Golden and Jon F. Merz for taking the opportunity to chat with me a while.

I always owe thanks to my family and friends, and I can never leave them out of an acknowledgement. If I did — hell, they'd hang me for sure. So to those people: Theresa Conte-McGee, Karin Conte, Diedre Finney, (and Luka, Shaq, Misty, Snow & Whisper), MaryAnn Ritacco, Joseph & Theresa Kwiatkowski, Anthony, Fran, Mia, Allessondro & Gabriella Conte; Jennifer Swindell, Ash Roland, Sarah Martin, Maggie Borneman, Adam Huber, Jimmy Gillentine, Cassie Lee, Liz DeJesus, Shannon Richards and many others.

I also need to give appreciation for the music of such

artists as: Brad Paisley, Emerson Drive, Bon Jovi, Jason Aldean, Billy Currington, Blue County, Chris Cagle, Clay Walker, Craig Morgan, Daughtry, Drew Davis Band, Little Big Town, Mark Wills, Tim Rushlow, Taylor Swift and many others for the keep-awake music at four in the morning to make sure this novel gets completed at all hours of the night.

All the folks at the HWA, NEHW and SHWA

And one final thanks needs to go out.

To you, dear reader. Whether I sell one or one million, someone somewhere is reading my books. Someone somewhere is keeping me doing what I love to do. For that, I cannot thank you enough.

"If you're going through Hell, keep on going.
Don't slow down. If you're scared don't show it.
You might get out before the devil knows you're there."

— Rodney Atkins

# I

The first thing Rebecca said was, "We got a stiff."

"What?"

"A dead body."

"Great! It's way too early for this crap," Jack said, wiping sleep from his eyes and seating himself on a wooden bench between rows of lockers.

"Black and whites are already on the scene," she said.

Jack looked down at his watch, "call them back and tell them we have eight more minutes until our shift starts." He yawned in that high-pitched way that he sometimes did purposefully to annoy Rebecca.

"Be serious."

"I'm always serious," he said, rolling his eyes. "And besides, what happened to the good ole days when we used to have cop chit-chat?" asked Jack, "First you would say, 'Good morning Detective Stoughton.' Then I'd say, 'Good morning, and how are you, Detective Strong?' Then you'd say, 'I'm good. How about you?' And then…"

"I'll have to remember that tomorrow morning," she smiled. Then a frown crossed her face. "It seems to be another case like Tuesday's."

"Tuesday was a suicide."

"Yes it was, but more of those handprints were found."

Jack stood in the clean-cut police squad room with his overcoat hung around his shoulder, like a mobster carrying a dead body. A large duffel bag full of supplies for out in the field hung around his other shoulder: extra ammunition for his Glock

1

and Rebecca's Beretta, a couple sets of cuffs, mace, and latex gloves; the usual assortment that he carried with him everyday on his job.

A puzzled look appeared on his face. He wasn't surprised that there was another murder. He was a homicide detective in a highly populated suburb, and just like everywhere else, murder and violence waited at nearly every corner. Maybe this was a suicide. He hoped so. But if it was a homicide, they might be forced to re-open Tuesday's case. There were no distinguishing marks or any type of personal souvenirs taken from the residence — or from the body to indicate a serial killer was on the loose. Then again, two deaths did not necessarily indicate that it was a psychopathic killer hunting down victims like something from a cop-novel. And he hated re-opening a closed case file. That would mean he'd been wrong. He was a decent man, but oh God, did he hate to be wrong.

It reminded him of his rookie year on the force. His first case he had ever gotten was a traffic violator and he was wrong about that, too. That was a bad day, he thought. He had pulled over the wrong car, and for a whole six months not one cop had eased up on him about it. No joke went unheard; not one sarcastic comment left unsaid.

"Better put your coat back on," said Rebecca. "It's even colder than yesterday."

"Yes, mother." Jack replied sarcastically and shrugged his leather trench back on. He took his Glock 17 from his locker and firmly placed the holster around his belt, snapping the strap closed on his right hip. Then he put the combination lock securely back into place through the metallic slot.

He wore his badge on a chain around his neck, and he had one pair of cuffs in their holster in the back of his belt. He was ready. *Let's go get the bad guys*, that's what he always said.

Rebecca took the lead and headed to the parking garage

to pick up their vehicle for the day. Jack was right behind her, but stopped to take a powdered donut from Mason Oliver's desk. The kid wouldn't mind, Jack figured. It's customary police food anyway.

Rebecca stood in front of the caged-glass window, speaking to a uniformed officer. He handed her a set of keys. It looks like the red one today, Jack thought. He—like Rebecca—had been hoping for the blue car. The blue Acura TSX was a nice ride and only had a few years on it; comfortable seats and plenty of leg room, unlike the red Nissan Altima they were assigned today. But this wasn't a rent-a-car center, and they had to take what was given to them.

Jack waived at the kid behind the glass and walked out the steel retracting door. "I'll drive, if you want."

"Sure," said Rebecca, tossing him the keys and sliding into the passenger side.

Jack popped the trunk and tossed the duffel bag in on top of a couple of bulletproof vests and a twelve-gauge shotgun, then closed it back down.

* * *

When they arrived, Jack was the first to get out. The chilly air was forceful, pushing him back towards the car, whipping at his face; cold, hard, and ruthless. Then Rebecca climbed out of the passenger side and shut the door. She heard the lock click in place behind her as she eyed the landscape.

Four patrol cars were situated at the curb, opposite the red sedan. Two of them had their flashers on, but no sirens whistled aloud.

It was one of those cold, dank days where you wanted nothing more than to sit at home by the fireplace with a good book; that was something that Jack loved to do: read a good cop novel, sip on some coffee, and relax in his recliner. It was the tranquil environment Jack would have rather been in..

They walked over to the house looking like a rendition of *Mulder and Scully*, walking side by side with all-business expressions on their faces.

The grey clouds were thinning. Soon, Jack thought, the sun would be out, making a glimmer of hope that the snow storm scheduled for the weekend wouldn't come true. They were forecasted for up to two feet. A new cloud front seemed to be moving in. Stronger, fiercer looking weather approached.

The house was a bit old-fashioned, as were most of the houses in the neighborhood. It was sky-blue vinyl-sided with white shutters and white painted stairs leading to the wraparound porch that held a swing on one end. Had the neighboring houses not been so crowded, one might think it was from a movie or a *Nicholas Sparks* novel, perhaps. A half-foot of snow remained in the yard with a single shoveled path, which abutted the snow-strewn driveway.

On the stoop stood a short and pudgy police officer with thinning hair and wrinkles on his face. His hands were shoved deep in the pockets of his navy work pants to keep them from the bitter cold. Frozen breaths formed in front of his mouth, then vanished into nothingness.

Jack knew all of the cops in Snow Hill and some in the surrounding towns and cities. Jack was a power-cop. He was nothing but the law, although he'd made an occasional fracture in it himself by speeding or going through a red light every once in a while. But aside from that, he was all about arresting the bad guy and cleaning up the streets a little.

Snow Hill wasn't solely about crime. It had its good points, too. It was a suburban haven in some aspects. There were streets filled with half-million dollar homes, the school system was one of the best in the state, and it was a small enough township where everyone knew almost everyone.

"Hey Randy," Jack said, puffs of breath forming in front of him. "How bad is it?"

"One of the worst, Jack," Randy Holms said. "My guess is that some crazy son-of-a-bitch went on a rampage. But hey, you're the detective."

Randy nodded his head, "Hello, Detective Strong." His round face would have been almost cute had it not been for the fact that he was pushing fifty and losing his hair.

"Hey," Rebecca said, now starting to shiver from the cold.

Jack smiled. "I'm Jack and she's Detective Strong?"

"Well, you have to earn respect, Jacky-boy," the old man joked.

"Don't make me break your hip," Jack laughed anxiously.

Randy knew he was joking, of course. Jack had never hated a cop in his whole life. He respected the hell out of them. To him, no matter what kind of an asshole someone was, everyone was the same when they threw on the uniform and clipped a badge to their chest.

"Hey Jack," a tall black man said, walking out of the house with a silver clipboard in hand.

"How's it going, Marty?"

"Decent," he said. "My stomach's a little knotted right now."

"How bad is it?"

"Come see for yourself," Marty said and turned around. He walked inside and headed for the stairs that sat just a few yards away from the porch entrance.

Jack and Rebecca quickly donned booties and followed Marty into the warm atmosphere of the house.

The stairs were carpeted in oyster grey, as was the hallway. The second floor looked small, but was actually quite large. It was split into three bedrooms. One was carpeted in a dark blue with the walls in a light sea green. It was clearly the children's bedroom with the bunk bed and toys scattered around. Another was dressed a little too feminine, Jack thought—probably a guest room. The master bedroom, where Marty Williamson was leading them, had a similar pea carpet as the guest room. However, it was stained with blood smears and imprints of mud left behind from the tracks of shoes.

Marty stepped aside, allowing ample space for Jack and Rebecca to walk through without trampling any evidence.

In the far corner of the room, inches away from the master bathroom, was the victim. He was sprawled out with eyes wide and dead. The man was in his work clothes: blue dress pants, a button-down shirt, and a tie that was not yet done.

"What's the deal with the vic?" Jack asked Marty.

"His name is Craig Long. He's a divorce attorney. One wife, two kids." Marty walked in the room behind Rebecca, who stood mostly still, wrenching her head around the room like a ferret. "Dispatch got a hang-up to this address a half-hour ago, and sent it out over the radio," Marty explained. "I was just down on Wilshire, so I picked it up. Came to the front door. Knocked twice," he imitated with an invisible door. "No answer. Then I tried the doorknob and it opened. I drew my piece. Identified myself twice. Then I found this guy two minutes later."

"Witnesses?" Rebecca asked, still eyeing the room.

"None that we could find," Marty said. "Courtney Long, the wife, was at work; the two kids were at school. I sent Steven Wilcox and Deborah Cruise to ask the neighbors if they heard anything before they left to pick up the family. They said no one saw a thing. They should be back in fifteen."

*Great*, Jack thought. Now he'd have to deal with the sobbing widow. He didn't mean to seem cold or heartless, but he would feel such sympathy for the wife and kids of the victims that he too would shed a tear; it would more often than not distract him from his job. And by the looks of it, his job couldn't start just yet. He needed to call Hugh Willmon, the department's forensics expert, to come down and take some samples of the mud trails and blood, sweep the room for fibers; anything that could assist in finding this man's killer. The smallest detail could result in an identity.

Jack stepped carefully over the body and squatted down by the man's face. He had some sort of contusion below the right brow; tiny puncture wounds filled his face, as if they were part of a connect-the-dot puzzle. The vic's throat had taken a deep slice. Flaps of his stomach were peeled open through his blood-soaked shirt. There were three clear slices in his skin, rippling the loose flaps open, revealing his insides. That was probably the cause of death. Unless the cuts on his face proved to be anything more meaningful than just battle bruising; then the COD might be different. Jack was almost certain that the cause of death was some sort of knife wound to the stomach and throat. Jack wasn't an expert in anatomy, but he was sure he could see the victim's liver and intestines; and a lung protruded out through the blood-matted tissue.

"Rebecca," Jack said, "give a call to Hugh Willmon. We need to get some samples back to the lab.

Rebecca reached in the right pocket of her denim jeans, pulled out her cellular phone, and fumbled through her digital phonebook for Hugh Willmon's number.

Marty was still waiting by the door, staring blankly at Jack, nervous, as if he were waiting for further instructions from the detective. Marty had made sergeant about eight months ago, but Jack had rank on the scene. However, Jack was never the type to give an order unless all hell was breaking loose. Fortunately, hell never did break loose for Jack.

Hell did break loose for this poor bastard.

"Got any gloves on you?" Jack asked Marty.

From his back pants pocket, Marty tossed over two unused latex gloves.

Marty Williamson always kept spares in his pocket for just an incident as this one. But knowing Jack as well as anyone could know Jack, Marty knew he had a box or two of unopened gloves in the trunk of his car, along with a duffel and everything else. He even thought he had seen Jack with an M5 at one point. Jack had a motto, "if the bad guys don't play by the rules, why should we?" It was a controversial saying, but true. Jack's Glock held sixteen rounds in the clip and one in the pipe, while an M5 clip held thirty or forty (depending on the length). It's a little hard to shoot back with a handgun that expels one round at a time while someone has an AK-47 that shoots five or six rounds per second. An M5 was legal for law enforcement use, but it was used only by tactical teams for undercover drug stings and serving warrants.

Jack slid on the gloves and pressed the vic around the jaw area. A bright green substance dribbled out of the tiny holes on his face, raining down to the olive carpet, producing a pure green, the truest green Jack had ever seen. So bright and lifelike. He dabbed his forefinger in one of the small puddles and felt it. Warm and greasy. He held it to his nose; it was odorless—the only scent was the latex glove.

Another officer walked into the room, Paul Wizter. Everyone called him Wiz or Wiz kid, although he wasn't a kid; he was pushing forty while Jack was nearly a decade younger. His face was pasty and frail, looking as if he were over the hill already. It was a side effect of smoking cigars since the age of seventeen, joining the force, and single-handedly taking care of his family. He seemed out of place in his uniform, Jack often thought, and Rebecca agreed. He should be in plain clothes with the gold badge symbolizing his rank. The silver badges were for officers, corporals, and sergeants. Everyone else from detectives to lieutenants to captains got the gold. And Jack often wondered if Tim Sutton got a platinum badge or not. He was the Chief of the Snow Hill Police Department, so perhaps he did.

"Hey Wiz," said Jack. "We got Hugh and a forensic team on the way."

"All right," he said. "A small crowd is gathering around outside."

"Awesome," Jack said sarcastically. "Now they'll have something to talk about at the dinner table tonight." Jack rose to his feet, watching his footing ever so carefully, and exited the room.

Rebecca was in the upstairs hall, examining the other two bedrooms. Nothing seemed out of place. The guest bedroom with the floral wallpaper and matching bed looked untouched, neat and odorless. The children's room had a red steel bunk bed with blue sheets and a corner desk at the far end filled with Legos and toy soldiers; the room was as clean as it could get with two young children. It smelled faintly of *Febreze* that the mother probably used to keep the smell of childhood play to a minimum.

No place other than the master bedroom seemed to be touched by an intruder, so Jack left the downstairs and examined both doors, front and back. Neither had splintered wood, a dinged base, or any other signs for forced entry; windows were intact downstairs and up. This meant that it was possible that the victim knew the killer.

Jack wandered around the living room waiting for Hugh and his team of three to show up in that great big white van of his.

On the oak mantelpiece, several pictures of this man's family glistened. They seemed too happy and full of life to think that the wife could commit such a heinous act. But one of the things that they teach you in police training is that the spouse is a suspect unless proven otherwise.

From what Jack could see of the body, there were no bullet holes, unless they had penetrated the chest and ripped him to shit. The killer was up close and personal; an act of jealousy, rage, or something else equally sinister. Jack pondered a dozen genuine scenarios in his head, playing them like a reel to his favorite movie with different epilogues, a white van showed up with blue lights flashing from the windshield and back doors.

Jack met Hugh outside and took notice of the couple dozen onlookers trying to get a glimpse of detectives or dead bodies, something to gossip about tonight.

It's funny how death and a god-awful crime could attract such an audience.

"What do we got Jack?" asked Hugh.

"A dead male. Mid-thirties with lacerations to the face and throat, deep gashes to his abdomen," said Jack, "and some green substance seeping through his cheeks."

"We better go take a look then," Hugh said, toting an oversized duffel bag filled with gloves, glass bottles of a dozen sizes, swabs, and special liquids to test for methamphetamine and cocaine; but narcotics didn't seem to be in play with this one.

Three members of the forensic unit in matching blue jumpsuits walked behind Hugh. The first was Janet Dietiz, a woman with the stomach for guts and blood, Jack supposed. He'd never seen her turn away from death in the two years he'd known her. Marcus Fryer was next and then Jay Buford, a young kid who looked like he should still be in high school. Jay had his very expensive crime scene camera strapped around his neck. Jack wasn't too familiar with cameras, but something like that went for a good fifteen hundred bucks, if not more.

"Fellas," Jack said, "up the stairs, bedroom on the left."

Jack followed behind Jay, climbing the stairs again.

There, Rebecca slouched against the wall, just past the guardrails to the stairs in the small open hallway. Her expression was blank and dry, as if she were a mere mannequin on display at *Macy's*: Her hands were stuffed in her pockets; her chest was the only thing moving, her lungs filling up with air and then releasing with a quiet sigh.

Jack walked up to her, "Are you okay?"

It took a second for Rebecca to acknowledge his presence. "Yeah," she said. "I'm fine. Just thinking about things."

"Anything you want to talk about?" Jack asked in less than a whisper, low enough that Rebecca was the only one to hear him.

"Not here," she said, "not now."

Jack took that to mean that something was seriously amiss. Rebecca had never been the tranquil type to just let things build up to where she didn't feel like doing her job, or at least pretending to do her job. Jack didn't think that it had anything to do with their little squabble last night. All couples have their fights, and to be honest, Jack couldn't remember the start of it, anyway. Perhaps the scene was too much for her. This was their eighth or ninth case in a row. Snow Hill, Massachusetts was never a syndicate of crime and murder, which was a little peculiar. It didn't have Boston's population or even Worchester's; somewhere close to eighty thousand, according to the census back in 2006. It was a small city, but even for that size, crime should be a little higher than it was. Jack wasn't complaining but he often wondered how he'd deal with it if he did work in Boston or Worchester. Would he be the man he is today? Or would the dozens of murders and drug busts and prostitution stings and warrant servings and car chases have gotten to him?

It was just before nine o'clock in the morning when a

cruiser pulled into the driveway on the right side of the house in back of a beige Lincoln Town Car that probably belonged to the victim upstairs. That side of the house was lined with azalea bushes. On the other side was a sloped embankment ten feet down, stretching out into another piece of land suitable to build an equally-sized house between the victim's and his neighbors, who were probably gathering in the front trying to get a glimpse of whatever was happening.

Jack looked on as Steven, a twenty-eight year old officer with a sandy mustache and growing stubble, got out of the driver's seat and opened the back door for Mrs. Long and her two children. She was clutching them for dear life. She kept her head down, avoiding the strong wind and the throng of onlookers. The children seemed more scared than upset, which was natural. By the looks of it, they were about five and eight. Each had a haversack secured by vinyl straps to their back. It was a hard thing for Jack to watch: a weeping widow and two newly fatherless sons.

Right about then a news van sporting a WBZ 4 Boston logo pulled up and parked across the street. Jack was not in the mood to deal with the press today. He'd let Marty handle that department.

This was a living reason of why Jack chose this career. To put murderers who take so much from innocent people behind bars for life, if not longer.

Mrs. Long, with the two children still clutched to her side, walked through a shoveled path in the snow to the steps of the wraparound porch.

"Mrs. Long," Jack said, and then paused briefly, allowing her to reach the top of the porch, "I'm Detective Jack Stoughton."

She didn't respond. She walked past Detective Stoughton as if he was invisible. She moved as if nothing in the world existed anymore. And to her, nothing did.

Jack followed behind her, attempting to communicate through her loud cries. "Mrs. Long, would you like me to get you some water?" Jack offered.

This time she did respond. "No," she cried, shaking her head in accordance.

Mrs. Long took a seat at the kitchen table that sat centered in the kitchen, surrounded by a beautiful architectural work of cabinets, counters, and rather pricy appliances, all in matching stainless steel. The two children stood next to their mother; the youngest began to shed tears, and his older brother joined in the chorus of loud wails.

Jack looked on in annoyance, but knew how she must feel. The same way Rebecca had felt so long ago.

Jack knew he wasn't going to get any questions answered just yet. It'd be quite some time before this group calmed down. Until then, Jack had his job to do.

He walked upstairs, finding Rebecca still standing where she had been when Jack had left her; she was in a different position this time, but with that same blank gaze at the eggshell walls of the hallway.

Bright flashes bounced off the walls, like lightning flickering repetitively, slicing through the air. It was Jay's digital camera. He uploaded photos to his laptop right then and there, sending them to the crime lab where someone on the receiving end would be waiting. It averaged out to around seventy or eighty pictures of close-ups and landscapes. Different angles, different zooms to capture the most minuscule piece of evidence that could potentially be the most important.

Jack walked to the door of the bedroom and peered in. Hugh was on one knee swabbing up that green goop that squeezed through the cuts on the victim's face, and then putting it inside one of his glass containers of evidence and sealing it securely in that tote bag of his. Meanwhile, Jay Buford started photographing the bathroom at different angles.

Jack hadn't paid attention to the bathroom at all. He wanted to wait until the evidence was collected before snooping around, looking for any clues, and picking which scenarios he liked best for this particular crime.

Hugh looked up from the body and noticed Jack. "I think I got the COD for you, Jack."

"What is it?" Jack asked, easing between Marty and Whiz.

With rubber gloves, Hugh held it aloft: "An open razor sliced his throat and jammed in his larynx. If I had to make a hypothesis right now, I'd say that was what did it, but I won't know for certain until we get the body back to the lab."

"Okay," Jack smiled in appreciation and walked back to the hall.

Rebecca was walking down the stairs. "I need some fresh air," she told Jack.

"I'll be here if you need me," said Jack. He looked at her intently, as if to see whether Rebecca would faint while walking down the stairs, but she did no such thing. Her lips were tight, her eyes loose and dreary. The cold air might do her some good, Jack thought.

Thankfully, the corpse had only been sitting for an hour or so. Had it been a few days that fulminous stench that often lingers with decomposing bodies would have filled the house in no time. Plus, being here so close to the murder meant there was a better chance to find evidence left behind.

Jack thought about speaking to the widow now, but he could still hear her sobbing all the way through a closed door, another wall, and up the stairs. She wasn't ready. Jack could wait. There was still a lot to be done. Hugh and his team needed maybe another thirty minutes to do their investigation in the master bedroom. The Coroner's office would come, package up the body, and ship it back to the lab. And Jack still had to go through a list of suspects. The first thing he thought of was the deceased's clientele.

As a lawyer, you're bound to have a share of grievances from the men and women you represent. Perhaps a client went too far. Next would be business associates. With no forced entry and valuables left behind, it didn't look like a robbery. More like something got out of control in the heat of anger — or passion.

Hugh and his team took their samples and left for the station to examine the body and the evidence more thoroughly. Rebecca was still outside getting air, talking to Randy Holms. Talking erratically about anything and everything as Becca tended to when she got anxious about something.

Jack walked back into the room where the blood stain still remained. He got on his knees, and with a chrome flashlight, glanced under the bed. Jack found a cordless phone, the phone with which the vic probably dialed 911. Hugh must've missed this, Jack thought, and with his forefinger and thumb, pulled it out by the antenna and plopped it on the green-blue bed sheets. He had to get a paper bag for it from the trunk of the sedan and bag it has evidence.

Blood smears washed the walls in the bathroom. There were dark maroon handprints on the mirror over the pedestal sink. Drops of blood spotted the floor from the bathtub at one end to the door and out into the bedroom where the victim had fallen to his death.

*It started in the bathroom,* Jack pondered in his mind. *And his wife slashed his throat from behind.* But it couldn't be. No. A woman who killed her husband wouldn't be crying like that, would she? And Mrs. Long was supposedly at work. Jack would get statements from her coworkers later to confirm that she was there at the approximate time of death. She seemed too loving and happy in those pictures over the fireplace to be the murderous kind; but it's all kinds that do the unthinkable act. In this case, Jack thought it was safe to rule her out as a prime suspect for the time being.

Jack started running through notions in his mind again.

*A friend, close relative had an argument with him in the bathroom; they were waiving their hands and it was an accident. But that doesn't explain the cuts on his face, and the fact that the open razor was jammed in his throat and his stomach was peeled open like an aluminum can.*

A spray of blood painted the white sink and the blue bathroom rug horseshoed around the toilet. *That's where he was standing when it happened.* Jack placed his feet where he thought the victim would have stood and tried to retrace his steps exactly.

"All right," Jack said to himself, "he cut his throat right here, while looking at the mirror. He grabbed his throat, which would explain his blood-soaked shirt; got dizzy; and placed one hand on this wall," Jack touched the wall where the handprint was, and then continued as if he were dizzy himself, wobbling about, gasping for air, reaching out for life that was not there, as Craig Long undoubtedly did. "And boom," Jack said. "He fell dead."

The door.

Jack had failed to notice it before. Two handprints burned into the woodwork of the bathroom door. Jack ran his gloved fingers over them, feeling the roughness and eyeing it ever so closely. It was the same thing that had been etched into the last victim's bedroom wall. Jack thought it was the work of a wood-burning tool, but something so exact couldn't be done in that little time. It was only about fifteen minutes from the time that the hang-up got reported to Marty's arrival at the scene. Maybe a half-hour. The print was so small and petite, like a handprint from an infant, and it only had three fingers and a thumb.

Jack took out the notepad that he kept in his right inside

pocket with the ballpoint pen clipped to the spirals. He jotted down obvious and not so obvious things. Little scenarios and possible suspects. Judging from where the murder took place and the fact that no forced entry was detected, it was safe to say that it was not a client, but a friend or family member. Jack didn't know too many lawyers who would invite clients over before eight in the morning to watch them shave, shit, and shower.

Back to the wife.

Jack did one more scan of the adjoining bedrooms and the small hallway that lay beside the stairs. No other signs of struggle or intrusion. Nothing seemingly out of place.

Back downstairs, the woman's tears seemed to have subsided. She looked at Officer Cruise with such befuddlement that it was safe to say Mrs. Long thought this to be a dream. A horrible nightmare that she couldn't wake herself from. The sad reality was that this was a nightmare, one as real and harsh as the cold wind outside. More brutal and devastating than a tropical storm. Her life would forever be altered.

Jack walked into the well-lit kitchen. The morning sun shined brightly through the half-dozen windows. Courtney Long sat at the table with a half-filled glass of water.

"Where are the kids, Deb?" Jack asked.

"In the living room," the officer answered.

"Good," said Jack. "Can you give us a minute, please?"

"Sure," she said, and exited the kitchen from the entrance near the stairs and the front door.

Jack walked over, pulled a chair out from underneath the table, sat down, and smiled sympathetically. "Mrs. Long," Jack said in a soft tone, "I need to ask you some questions."

She nodded.

"Did your husband have any enemies?" Jack asked. "Anyone that might want to hurt him? Friends or family?"

She shook her head, "No."

"Any clients of his that maybe ..."

"Wait a minute!" she interrupted. Her eyes lit up and widened as if she'd remembered a long-forgotten memory. "There was this guy at the club a couple nights ago," she said. "I don't know what happened, but Craig got really mad at him."

"Did they get into a physical fight?"

"No," she said, her eyes welling up. "They just argued. I don't know about what. I think about money."

"Which club was this?" Jack asked and got out his pad and pen.

"The country club," she said. We've only been members for a few weeks now," Mrs. Long explained. "We got this postcard in the mail," Courtney Long got up from her seat, and on top of the refrigerator was an irregularly-sized postcard. It was yellow and blue with black writing. It opened up like an envelope and read:

*Mr. & Mrs. Long,*

*The Snow Hill Country Club invites you to become its newest members.*

*At this exciting time, we have just redesigned our facilities with a new tennis court and new swimming pool. This is a special, once in a lifetime offer.*

*Sign up today and use reference number: NMSHCC216*

A picture of a tennis court, swimming pool, and a door that read STEAM ROOM lined the postcard. There was also a man in butler outfit, with arms wide open, a snippy grin, and faded grey hair, with a bubble overhead that read "WELCOME!"

"So, do you think that this man your husband had this altercation with could have done this?"

"I don't know," she cried. "I don't know," she repeated, and once more, "I don't know."

Courtney Long looked shaky and frail. Jack grabbed her arms to steady her and walked her back to her chair. "I'm going to go talk to this man," Jack promised. "Do you know his name?"

She shook her head, unable to speak.

"What does he look like?"

She pointed to that butler on the thick cardboard with the eighty-seven cent postmark on it.

"He's the host?"

She nodded again.

"I'm going to leave a patrol car outside for a little while, and some more detectives are going to come in and examine the scene once more," explained Jack. "I'm going to go talk to this man."

Jack walked away from the kitchen, noticing that Courtney Long had placed her head on the table, crying in such pure horror no person should ever have to go through.

He took his cell phone from his left inside pocket and dialed for Walter Martinez. It rang twice.

"Martinez," he answered.

"It's Jack," he said.

"What's going on?"

"Can you and Walters come over and check out this scene?" Jack asked. I have a lead and need to check it out A-SAP."

"Sure, Jack," Martinez agreed. "What's the address?"

"One-eighteen Alpine Street," Jack told him.

"We'll be there in fifteen," Martinez said and hung up.

Jack followed the grey carpet down the hall and outside to the door that was ajar. Rebecca was standing there with a cigarette between her lips. "'Becca, you quit smoking, remember?" Jack placed one hand on his hip.

"Special occasion," she said, taking a drag and sticking the cigarette between her middle and fore-fingers.

Jack shrugged it off, knowing he would get into an argument with her if he didn't. Smoking was one of the worst things you could ever do around Jack Stoughton. Rebecca had been good for almost a full year; never used a patch or any special gum, just quit as she promised Jack. Something had really gotten to her to get her to light one up again.

"We need to go," Jack said to Rebecca. "We've got a lead to follow." He turned his focus to Randy, "Martinez is coming down to finish up here."

"Okay Jack," Randy said.

Rebecca flicked the cigarette into the snow, extinguishing the tip. She walked behind Jack to their car and slid back into the passenger side. Jack took the keys from his pocket, opened his own door, and turned the ignition on.

It was one of those bitter mornings when frost cluttered the windows in a matter of minutes and you needed to warm up the car for it to melt and create a bearable atmosphere inside. It had to be pushing the high teens this morning, and with the afternoon it might rise to twenty to twenty-five degrees, but that was being a little too generous.

The Snow Hill Country Club was only a ten minute drive. It was luxurious on the outside, and more so in the interior. It was a tall building that stretched far back on acres of land, with a golf course and a pair of tennis courts in the back. They had members come from all over the state to their Swedish spa. It even had enough funding to advertise on television during the five o'clock news. Most of the members of this organization paid dues quarterly or yearly. It had a lot of support from wealthy men who liked to chase golf and tennis balls.

The front of the entrance had a rectangle of frosted glass to the left of the heavy steel door that sat under an adobe roof. Jack and Rebecca got out of their car; badges hung from their ball chains around each of their necks, dangling in the cold, frost caking on the metal almost instantly.

Jack pulled on the satin-nickel door handle, but it wouldn't move. A black slot on the left side of the door jamb stuck out a quarter of an inch with a green light indicator on it showing that it worked.

Jack remembered seeing a key card in one of the evidence bags that had headed down to the station with Hugh to be further examined for hair fibers and prints. A doorbell with the same finish as the door handle sat just above the key card holder. Jack pressed it once, then twice, then a third time, this time longer than the last two. In his peripheral vision, Jack saw a small surveillance camera pointed at an angle with the doorway as its mark.

No doubt that security staff, or whoever monitored those cameras, were watching Rebecca and Jack right now as they waited for someone to open the door.

"How can we help you," a voice said through a hidden intercom.

Rebecca flashed her badge to the camera. "Police officers. We need to speak to you."

"One second, please," the monitor's voice said.

A second later the door opened with a soft *buzz*. Jack pulled back on the handle, and allowed Rebecca to walk in first to a small room, with no more space than you'd find in a parking lot ATM vestibule. Next, they opened a solid oak door, and found themselves in the grand foyer of the country club. Neither Jack nor Rebecca had ever been there before, and it was a luxurious sight. It was lavished with a thin, dark blue carpet with a maroon diamond pattern. Chairs of every size in beige fabric lined the cherry wood walls where paintings of local artists gave it a reputable look. An arched counter sat a couple yards away with a man in brown suit and matching tie sitting behind it, staring at Jack.

Jack could see a glow from underneath the top counter of the desk. It was where the monitors sat, discrete and hidden.

"How may I help you two officers?" The man behind the counter asked, then sipped his mug of coffee.

Rebecca walked up to him first. "We need to talk about one of your members, Craig Long."

"I believe I remember him," the man said. "Did he do something wrong? If he did we may have to revoke his membership."

Rebecca read is name tag pinned to his lapel: G. Gabibelli. "Mr. Gabibelli, Craig Long was murdered early this morning. We have reason to believe that he got into an argument with one of the employees here not too long ago. Do you recall anything about that?" Rebecca was firm and relentless with the questioning as she always was. As soon as she posed one inquiry another two surfaced her mind.

The man's expression indicated he had no knowledge of his murder, and although Rebecca thought momentarily that it could be some sort of conspiracy within the boundaries of this club, but that thought vanished as quickly as it entered her mind.

Mr. Gabibelli was an older man, more or less pushing sixty. His hair was grey and thinning all over. He wore glasses that made him look like a seventh-grade nerd who had just won first place in the school's science fair.

"I'm sorry, but no complaints like that were ever brought to my attention," he said. "Let me get the floor manager down here. Maybe he knows something about it," he said kindly.

"Okay," she nodded, backing away from the desk and going to stand by Jack. "What do you think?" she whispered

"This lobby would make a nice living room," Jack said.

"Be serious," Rebecca said.

He could tell in her tone that she meant it. Jack stroked the stubble on his face with his thumb and forefinger. His lips were tight, eyes taut. "I'm going to look around," he told her.

There were several doors in the foyer, all in the same dark wood as the one they had entered. There were three on the right, for the swimming pool, fitness/massage therapy, and restrooms respectively. A couple at the back were marked exit and restaurant. Three doors behind the arched marble desk weren't labeled, and Jack took that to mean it was for the employees only, although a red sticker with gold letters that read EMPLOYEES ONLY would have made it official.

A few minutes later, a man in an upscale navy suit emerged from the middle of the three unlabeled doors. He was young, younger than the receptionist by at least fifteen years. His mustache was neatly groomed and his teeth a pearly white.

"How may I help you officers?" the floor manager asked from behind the counter.

"We have reason to believe that one of your members, Craig Long, got into an argument with another member or employee here," said Jack.

"Do you know anything about that?" Rebecca chimed in.

"I believe I do." He scratched his neatly kept mustache. "It was with one of our bartenders over a dispute of payment."

"What kind of payment?" asked Jack.

"He and his wife ordered beverages that they thought were too pricey for them," he explained. "I got a phone call about it, and I waived the fees as a one-time courtesy to Mr. and Mrs. Long."

"Can we talk to the bartender?" Rebecca asked.

"I'm afraid he's not in today or tomorrow," the manager said.

"Can we get the address of the bartender, a name, or something?"

"Of course," he said. "Just give me a minute to get you the file." The manager walked back through the door he had entered, and returned a moment later with a manila folder, labeled THOMAS HOPKINTON. "Here you are officers. Hope this helps."

Jack took the file and shot back a grateful smile.

"And your name, sir?" Rebecca asked, her pad and pen in hand. Ready.

"George Miller," he said. He shook both their hands and walked them to the front door. "If there's anything else I can do, just ask." He smiled, then turned away.

"Thank you," Jack said, and followed Rebecca out of the country club.

Outside, a light shower of snow fluttered down. That nuisance stuff, as some people called it. The wind was still strong and fierce, stealing the heat right from their bodies.

Rebecca flipped through the file on the bartender, holding it tight from the wind. She was looking for his address. 121 Mercy Drive, it read on the third page, on the top portion of his work résumé. This man was twenty-eight and had only had two jobs. Worked at the country club for five years, it also read on the same page.

Jack thumbed the button on the key ring and unlocked both doors. He got in on the driver's side, and slid the keys into the ignition as Rebecca climbed in, putting the folder on the dashboard while she fastened her seatbelt, then picking through the papers again, trying to get a sense about who this man was.

The engine started with ease. The heat slowly came on to

full strength. Jack pulled away from the curb and drove off to find this potential suspect.

*Joseph McGee*

# II

Kyle wasn't paying attention to anything his teacher was saying. The bell was ten minutes away from ringing, from giving everyone on the third floor—and half of the second—a thirty-five minute break for lunch.

Mrs. Wrangler was in the midst of a long speech about the Civil War and things that had affected the war in early colonial America. She had the voice to turn anything exciting into the most boring topic.

Kyle was, more or less, giving his attention to Kennedy Jensen. She was the girl next door. Best friends with Kyle since third grade. They had found comfort in each other that neither could find in their other friends. The fact that they were so close made Kyle tempted to do a little more than just talk. He'd been hinting around for a while: the obvious staring and flirting, the way he'd look at her. He knew she knew. She had no objection to it thus far, and today would be the day. Yes. Today he would do it. At lunch. Behind the closed doors by where they served the free lunches and pizza and soda. Where no one could see them and rejection would be a little easier to take, he would ask her on a date.

*Me touching her*, he thought, along with more inappropriate things that shouldn't be passing through his mind in U.S. History.

Kennedy was beautiful. Gorgeous. Five-six, a hundred-twenty pounds. Brown hair, walnut eyes. A hair salon makeover. She sat in the fourth row, two seats from where Kyle sat in the last chair in the same row. She—like everyone else—was watching the clock over the blackboard. Now with three minutes until the bell, Mrs. Wrangler was giving out this weekend's homework assignment: a five-thousand-word essay on the conflicts of the Civil War from 1861 to 1865.

The noon bell rang its loud freedom cry. Classroom chairs emptied and the halls spilled out with students on the way to their lockers. Some would then head to the soda machine at the A-wing to grab a Coke; others would pass the vending machines and head out the back entrance for a quick drag from a cigarette. It was a popular hangout for smokers — and potheads.

Kyle walked over to his locker at the C-wing to retrieve his books for Earth Studies and Advanced Geology. He would save a few minutes now, rather than jerk away the time after lunch and be late. His Earth Studies teacher hated tardiness: Mr. Mitchell would cringe like some tough wrangler. His eyes would stare; his lips tight. Fierce. He would tell that poor soul to leave his room and not return until the next day. "If you don't wish to learn, get out of my class," he would say. That was his motto, and he stuck to it firmly.

Rachel Summers walked up to Kyle. Blonde hair falling just below her shoulders. Sapphire eyes. Slim body. Dressed in a white and blue uniform: Snow Hill High's colors. "Hey Kyle," she said, smiling at him endearingly.

"Hey Rach," he said, fumbling through his locker for the right books. He didn't need this right now. Some high school cheerleader looking for a good lay. He wasn't the rude type. He knew what Rachel wanted, and he did everything but bluntly tell her where to go and how to get there. His eyes were on another girl. A special girl. Kennedy.

She was the cheerleader all the guys wanted. She had the looks and that charisma to get almost anything she ever wanted. This was the time where she could cheat her way through life. All the male teachers took a liking to her, as they nonchalantly eyed her firm body that rounded at the perfect places; her breasts posing as hidden temples waiting to be explored.

"What's going on?" asked Rachel.

"Just getting my books," he said. Kyle showed her the covers for each of the subjects. If he carried out his idea of leaving early he wouldn't need them at all today. It wasn't really kosher to just skip out of school, but who'd miss him if he wasn't there? "I got to run to lunch," he smiled. "See ya later."

"Bye," she said, turning away and going back down the C-wing to the conjoining halls where a group of similarly dressed girls waited, giggling in a high-pitched annoyance.

Kyle paid no mind to them and headed down a flight of stairs that sat a row of lockers away, bringing him directly to the entrance to the cafeteria.

The table that he always sat at was at the end in the third row, closest to the stairs he'd come down and nearest to the set of doors that led out of school. He was still considering cutting out early. Driving home before the start of the snow storm that they had been predicting on the news all week. Kyle was concerned that if he left early Kennedy would have to walk home. Her parents wouldn't come to get her. God, no. That would be too easy and such a waste of time for parents to take time out of their day to ensure their only child was safe coming home after school.

Kyle had heard the snow storm they talked about was going to be a pretty nasty one. Up to two feet, possibly more; thirty-six degrees Fahrenheit at most, and it was supposed to drop way down over night. Freezing. Start up with more snow on Saturday and Sunday. It wasn't a bother for Kyle to give Kennedy a ride. None at all. She lived right next to his house. In the back on Roseward Street. Even if she lived across the city, Kyle would still make the effort to give her a ride there.

Kennedy's mother and father where the worst kind of parents to have. Her dad used to beat the hell out of her when he got drunk, and her mother didn't open her mouth to stop it. Never tried. That was her daughter for Christ's sake. How could any mother allow something so awful to happen to their own child? That's a question that had puzzled a lot of people through the years. Kyle understood, though. And he'd help her. Talk to her. Comfort her. Be a shoulder she could cry on, which happened more often than not. A million times Kyle wanted to go over there and rearrange that fucker's face. Hit him, as he'd been hitting on her all these years. Worse. As if he was possessed by some revenge demon, losing his ability to determine wrong from right. Not stopping until that fucker was *not* moving. Until he was *not* breathing.

After having a few slices of pizza from the cafeteria and washing it down with a Coke and catching up with his friends Bill Walker and Seth Serenduski, Kyle left as planned. It was about time, too. Seth was in the middle of one of his sex-jokes that often portrayed him, the funny one of the trio. He also had the looks that could make him a million dollars on a stage in Los Angeles: glasses, red hair, freckles. At five-eight, he was taller than *Tom Cruise*. Billy, on the other hand, was the kind of kid everyone got along with. He was popular. Funny. All the girls were attracted to him. He would always dress stylish, as if he were an *Abercrombie & Fitch* model.

Kyle always seemed out of place with those two. He was a starter for the high school basketball team. Mysterious and witty. Attractive with a physique like some professional athletes. Calm and neutral.

After he left school, he'd run around doing some errands before returning to give Kennedy a ride home. He stopped at the grocery store just a few blocks away from his house to pick up some last minute things before the snow storm touched down that night or this weekend. Milk and water and soda. Canned vegetables. Fruit. Spaghetti. Chicken. Meat. Packaged cookies and some other sweets. Batteries for his flashlight, in case the power were to go out. His order came to $87.58. He handed the cashier his bank card. She slid it through her machine, and the register printed a receipt for him. She smiled at him and placed the receipt gently in his hand. He signed his name to it and handed it back to her.

"Thank you," he said, pushing the cart out of the way for the next customer.

"Have a good day, sir," the cashier replied, despite Kyle being her age or younger.

It felt as though the temperature had dropped ten degrees from just the time that Kyle arrived at the store to the time he left, some thirty-odd minutes. And maybe it had.

His truck was parked in the second row, third from the last space to the right. It was the only nearby vacant space he'd seen. Around here, when they called for such an hellacious winter storm, men, woman and children ran to the store before it hit, as if it were going to snow ten feet and everything would be blocked away for a week. And if Kyle's memory served him correctly, there was a time that something just like that did occur. His grandfather had told him about this not too long ago. The blizzard of 1976. Something around five or six feet. Electricity was out for days; in some areas for weeks. People lost their lives in car accidents or just walking down the street.

Kyle thought if that ever were to happen again it wouldn't be for a while, and if it did, it would be pretty amazing to see such an event. Yes, it might take a couple of lives. Yes, it would bury him in his apartment for a week. But to see such a catastrophic storm would be incredible to him. He loved the snow. He loved winter. There was no explanation of any kind but it somehow brought him peace. Freedom. The joy of Christmas and the wildness of New Year's.

Kyle still had time to put away the groceries before he

had to return to school. He was riding on empty, too. He needed to stop at the gas station before picking up Kennedy, or he might not make it home at all.

He drove a Ford F-250 that his grandparents had bought for him six months ago when they won the state lottery. Over a hundred million dollars. They gave some to Kyle's parents and to his aunt and uncle. Kyle got five million out of the deal. He was hoping to save his money for college and then find a career he was interested in and buy himself a new house somewhere nice. Luxurious. Technologically advanced.

Kyle's likely career choice was in the military. His granddad had joined and retired, same with his dad. Both U.S. Army. Retired out as sergeants. Aside from creative writing, which never crossed his mind as a serious career, that was the only thing on his plate for the time being. He didn't exactly know how Kennedy fit into that plan.

He and Kennedy had been friends for almost eleven years. Yet Kyle wanted more. He was in love. He had never been in love before, but he believed this was it. Every time he looked into her eyes, the clouds in the sky disappeared. Touching her shoulder or grazing her hair sent him away to a foreign land. One where love and truth were all that mattered. He would love to go back there all the time, and every time he thought about it, he did. It was a place he'd want to live in forever.

For the past few months, Kyle had been hinting around. The obvious, blubbering kind of indicative phrases. She knew. He knew she knew. Kennedy seemed fine with it.

Kyle was eventually going to take a chance. Ask her to a movie. Invite her to dinner. Both. Or just take a long drive down to Hampton Beach in New Hampshire this summer. It wasn't a long drive, but they could stop at some panoramic vistas that were placed along the way. Stay at a fancy hotel on the beach. Spend time walking along the boardwalk hand-in-hand with other cute girlfriend-boyfriend combos. It was a nice thought, of course. A thought that entered his mind daily, like fingernails scratching the inside of his skull. *Scratch, scratch, scratch.* Memories of her throughout the years; daydreams of things that had never happened, and of future events that still lay dormant.

Kyle drove back to his house and parked at the end stretch of the long driveway that widened enough for two cars to park on either side. With a handful of grocery bags, Kyle shifted through his pocket for his keys and opened the door on the back side of the house where he resided in an in-law's apartment. Through the French doors, down a series of ten steps. He was greeted by Shadow, his dog of four years. A white and grey Alaskan malamute. Wagging his tail. Excited to see Kyle home early today. Panting back and forth. Nuzzling Kyle's palm as he walked past the dog and placed the groceries on the table that sat centered in the kitchen. To the right were the sink, dishwasher, counters and cupboards; on the left, an electric stove and a microwave hutch decorated with mail, catalogs, novels and the occasional scraps of papers.

He made two more trips to the truck to get the remaining food and put them in the fridge. After he finished putting everything away, Kyle stored the non-ripped plastic bags underneath the sink with the rest of his collection.

He looked at the microwave. The time read 1:21 P.M. He had a few minutes to kill before he had to leave. His spent a minute of that time going to the bathroom, and the rest he spent preparing some dog food for Shadow. A can of chicken and liver that, to him, smelled like someone already ate it and it had come out the other end.

He left Shadow eating. Back out to the cold.

The wind had settled a bit, and the sky had opened up. *Maybe it's not going to snow today after all.* Thinning clouds had dissipated, revealing the sun, its poisonous rays heating his black coat with the Boston Celtics logo stitched on the back in white and green thread. That new rookie they picked up during the draft proved to be useful for a number fourteen pick, and Paul Pierce was doing his usual: twenty-five plus points a game. *Best Celtics' player since Larry Bird*, he thought.

He climbed into the cab of his truck and started the ignition. It turned over smoothly. Purring. Exhaust lazily spiraling up in back.

His mom and dad hadn't come home from their jobs yet. They were both supposed to come home early today if the weather showed true. So far, it had not.

His dad worked at a private law firm downtown, and his mother managed an Italian restaurant in Worchester called Lavender Square. It was a purple brick square at the corner of Shrewsbury and Loyatte in what was called "Restaurant Row," an area lined with diners and cafés of all sorts. Italian. Greek. Irish. Man, did mom's place serve a decent meatball sub. Kyle would sometimes skip out of school to go eat there, but every time he did, he was a few minutes late for his next class. Maybe he'd call his mother and ask her to pick up a sub for him. Yeah. He could definitely go for one tonight. Nah. She probably left work already.

At a quarter 'till two, Kyle was waiting patiently by the snow-covered steps on the east side of the building. The bell rang and immediately eager students poured out the doors, looking to get home to start their weekend. At the same time, the sky opened up into something awful. Something cold. Stern. Violent. The wind was more powerful than ever. Whistling through the eaves on the neighboring houses across the street. Screaming at their windows, like all the hate in the world collaborating together for one struggling stance. Banging doors. Rattling shutters.

A flurry of snow fell. Light at first. Getting heavy until the flakes were the size of quarters. Covering the exposed parts of the sidewalk until everything was white. A perfect, blinding white, contrasting with the students wearing different-colored hoods and jackets and gloves and backpacks. Mixing in so elegantly for a winter's storm.

Kennedy came bursting through the door in an eggplant jacket and blue jeans, with plum snow boots that were just a shade off the color of her jacket. She greeted Kyle with a smile.

"Need a ride?" he asked, already knowing that she'd accept.

"Sure," she said, walking down the steps. "Where'd you park?"

"Over there." He pointed back a ways. Past the gate to the parking lot that bordered three streets: Clinton in front, Dartmouth to the right and Barry Road on the left. There, school buses were loading up with passengers and parents were picking up the freshman and sophomores.

Kyle walked with her, side-by-side, to his parking spot. Closest row to the front and three over from dead-center middle. It was the only spot available. The spot that he had made available earlier was already taken by a parent picking up his child.

Kennedy tilted her head far back, looking at the sky, as if to read the mind of Mother Nature and determine what type of storm this would be. She had a feeling that this was just the calm before the storm. And oh, what a storm it would be. If the meteorologist's prediction was somewhat founded, not too many people would be out tonight.

"Looks like it's going to be a good storm tonight," she paused, "and this weekend.

"Yeah, it does," Kyle agreed.

In the mere minutes that Kyle had left his truck to wait by the door for Kennedy, an inch of snow had accumulated on his windshield. He climbed into the cab and pressed the wipers on full speed to clear the snow, side-to-side, scraping the glass clear and leaving a residue of liquid.

"Have you heard anything more about the storm?" Kennedy asked. "I haven't heard anything about it since Wednesday."

"It's supposed to be bad," he told her. "They upped it to three feet; in some parts more." Kyle recalled hearing the newsman saying that on the radio as he made his way back to the high school. "Supposed to start now," Kyle shifted his head up, "and go off and on until Monday night, I heard."

"A big one, huh?"

"Yeah," he said. "I skipped out early to head to the grocery store before it started."

"At least you got food," she said.

Kyle sat in his truck, waiting for the school to vacate somewhat. He didn't want to be in a traffic jam in the parking lot of his school; some of these drivers were horrible. The roads were beginning to get slippery. It was just a mess all around. Waiting twenty minutes, rather than possibly denting his F-250, was a good call, he believed.

While they were waiting, the snow started coming down a little heavier. When only a few cars remained, Kyle shifted to reverse and pulled out. Shifted to drive and followed a green Subaru. He noticed a police car traveling south on Dartmouth Street, and he allowed him to go by before pulling out of the lot.

The cruiser put its blue strobes on and disappeared onto one of the side streets up ahead. Kyle continued straight until he came to a four-way stop, then turned right on to Elesworth. He made a left at the end onto Buresta Road. House number eighteen was his. He pulled into the driveway. His parents were still not home. He turned off the engine and pulled Kennedy's bag into the front cab for her. He left his books behind, not needing them. Kennedy would explain to him later what was going on in the classes he missed and if any work was due. And the way things were looking, school may be cancelled Monday. A nice three-day weekend, perhaps. Four was unlikely, but three was almost guaranteed.

He walked Kennedy to the back where the chain-link fence bordered their yards. Kyle threw the latch up on the door and kissed Kennedy on her soft cheek. *Only a few more inches to the left*, he thought.

"I'll see you later," she said.

"Yeah," he agreed. "Why don't you stop by for dinner in a few hours?" Kyle suggested.

"You cooking?" She asked.

"But of course." He smiled at her, looking into her eyes, trying to read her soul. They sparkled in dim rays of sunlight struggling to show themselves through the clouds, so perfect it made her look as though a thousand diamonds were falling from the heavens in flawless chaste.

Kyle watched Kennedy walk to her house and up the stairs, her book bag slouched over her shoulder. She went through the door, locking it behind her.

Then Kyle opened his own door. He brushed his hand back and forth to loosen the melting white flakes of snow caught in his hair. Shadow was waiting at the bottom of the stairs, wagging his tail as dogs do when someone they know and love has come back from the shortest *or* longest trip. Panting. Tongue hanging out.

"Hey boy." Kyle knelt down; scratching Shadow's back and belly; kissing him once, twice, three times on the forehead. Kyle kicked off his boots, producing water from the rubber tracks, and took off his jacket. He hung it on the mirrored coat rack that stood in the petite hall facing the stairs. It had an engraving on it of a pack of wolves isolated in the winter mountains.

His living room was of decent size. It had a couch and recliner in a matching almond color. A fifty-two inch television sat in front of the couch, some fifteen feet away. A movie collection, compact discs, and video games hung alphabetically on the cherry wood shelves that enclosed itself around the TV. A wall fountain hung on the far side next to the recliner. It was stone-colored with real granite placed here and there inside the water bowl for a more realistic feel. It made the room look more elegant and tasteful.

He plopped down on the cushioned couch for a little R & R before he had to cook dinner. And what should he make? He had a refrigerator full of food now. He could decide later. Kyle put his feet up on the couch, placed his head against the armrest that seemed to form comfortably around his head, and turned on the TV, flipping channels for special weather reports. And on the Weather Channel it read in block letters:

STORM WARNING FOR CENTRAL
MASSACHUSETTS. UP TO 36 IN.
FOR MOST AREAS. WIND CHILL -15°F.
STORM IN EFFECT UNTIL MONDAY 1 P.M.

It was going to be a big storm, indeed. Blocking Kyle's entranceway. Burying his truck. He'd be stuck in all weekend. Not such a bad idea. Some time to reflect and rest up. Movies to watch. Video games to play. Sleep to be had.

He pressed the power button on his remote, and turned the television off. He turned his body around, facing the couch, looking at blurs of brown. He closed his eyes for a short nap. He wasn't completely comfortable with his jeans still on but he was content. In a few minutes he dozed off into sleep. Into a dream.

*Boiling molten rock. Heated lava spreading around his house.*

*Melting snow. Melting tires. Thousands of people being taken out by a tidal wave of igneous rock. A voice whispering: "Snow Hill no more." And another voice: "We're back." Kennedy and a dozen other figures Kyle couldn't make out stood on a platform untouched by the lava. A borderland. They were shouting "Come here! Kyle, come to us! Hurry!" His arms were now in skeletal form. His body was being covered in a liquid coat of hot ash. A mountain of it came splashing onto him. Killing him.*

He woke up.

Perspiration was dripping down his brow, in his eyes and on his lips, and he could taste that bittersweet savor of sweat. He sat up from the couch like someone kicked him in the gut; his lungs inhaling and exhaling heavily.

Kyle never had such an intense dream before. He could feel the warmth of it. The fear. The pain. Then he opened his eyes, and all the sensations disappeared. It took a minute for his eyes to pool back into focus. He got off the couch, trying to shake off that terrible nightmare.

He had been asleep for nearly two hours. When he left the living room to scurry through the fridge for something to make, he saw a purple jacket hanging next to his on the coat rack in the small hall that bordered the living room, kitchen and front stairs.

It was Kennedy's.

Kyle wiped sleep from his eyes. "Kennedy?" He called.

The kitchen was empty. He looked past the kitchen to the narrow mocha-carpeted hall but found the bathroom empty. At the end stood the office/computer room. Also empty. He went through an archway and up the stairs that led up to the main house where his parents resided and to where his bedroom sat, and found Kennedy sitting on the bed, her hair strewn in a wild vortex. Shadow was in her lap, nuzzling her hand.

"Kennedy, are you okay?" Kyle had sleep in his voice, and she no doubt knew that he had been taking a nap. She had to let herself in with the spare key that he had given her years ago when she was having problems with her family. He had told her whenever she needed to get away from it all, she was welcomed here. Anytime. All the time.

When she lifted her head, Kyle froze. A new fury began to grow inside him. Her upper lip was swollen and cracked. Dry blood stained her nose. She didn't have to say a word. Kyle knew. "Are you okay?"

She nodded. Speechless.

Kyle went to his closet door next to the door leading to the bedroom. Inside was a folded up nylon duffel bag. He grabbed it and shut the door. "I'll be back," he said and walked out, not waiting for a response.

Kennedy didn't say anything. She knew what was going to happen, or at least had an idea. She sat there finding comfort in the dog and the way she felt for Kyle. She cried, as hard as she could. Those tears were like a torrent on a stormy night. Shadow, with a soft whimper, pushed himself up to her. Hugging her only as dogs can.

Kyle slipped on his sneakers that he had kicked off in the living room; he didn't bother to put on his jacket. His rage, his fury would keep him warm long enough to do what he had to do. Walking through his yard with a purpose. Snow crunching beneath the soles of his shoes. Up those cement steps to the door that had been left unlocked.

No one was in the kitchen, but a hot pan of something sat on the counter next to the sink, ready to be served for dinner. The kitchen led to the three bedrooms and a bathroom. At the conjunction of the hall and the kitchen sat a small group of stairs leading down into an excessively large living room and the front entrance.

Kyle didn't call for the father; he didn't call for Kennedy's mother; but went straight to the end of the hall, the room on the right: Kennedy's bedroom. Lilac walls. Oak furniture. They didn't quite match, but Kyle wasn't about to do a fashion arrangement. For a solid minute, Kyle floated from his body and watched himself taking clothes from the dresser and packing them messily in the bag. Underwear. Shirts. Pants. A belt. Pictures that she kept on top of the bureau of her and Kyle that summer two years back when she went to Disney World with him and his family. After clearing half of her clothes, Kyle found her notebook computer on a small work-center desk and placed it on top of the clothes. He used its eight-pound weight to compact the items enough for it to zipper shut. Kyle found her backpack resting on the doorknob of the closet door. He swung one of the straps around his shoulder and carried the larger bag in his left hand. Gripped tight. *This will be enough to hold her for a little*, Kyle thought, *until we can get new clothes and whatever else she may need.*

"You little bastard," said her father in a drunken slur from the living room.

The front of the kitchen opened into a balcony overlooking the living room. Kennedy's father forced himself up the stairs. "What the hell y-you think you're d-doing?" He had on a white tank top, commonly known as a "wife beater." Perfect match for him. Wife beater. Daughter beater. That and a pair a boxers that were cut too short and were semi-tight, revealing too much detail in a white trash manor. Looking like a slob of sorts. Oily hair, a week's beard.

Knowing the laptop would be shielded from any hard fall, Kyle let the bags drop. "Kennedy's staying with me for a little while."

"Wanna fuck her, ah boy?"

Kyle paid no attention to the man's crude comment. Using the railing for support, Kennedy's father walked to the kitchen. "Wanna stick your dick in that bitch."

Mrs. Jensen came from the bedroom down the hall in a

blue flannel nightgown. Her eyes were welling up, her cheeks swollen. She was a victim, too.

"Your daughter is staying with me for a while," Kyle told Kennedy's mother, staring into her eyes with such a strong gaze that it almost made her shiver.

"No, she is not," Mr. Jensen said. His words slurring together to form: "na-shes-nopt." He reached out to grab Kyle's arm forcefully, intending to knock him around as he did to his own daughter.

With an uppercut Kyle knocked his arm away. Then he spun around and landed a sidekick to the man's rib cage, knocking him to the hardwood floor and down a few steps, stealing the wind from his lungs. Ribs cracked. One or two. Three.

"Want to press charges?" He looked at Michelle Jensen. "Call the cops." He picked up the bags with one hand and left, gently closing the door behind him as a puff of white clouds forced their way inside.

He wanted to go back inside. There and then. Kick him. Punch him. Scream what a lousy father he was; a horrible human being. *A pathetic son of a bitch!* But Kennedy was more important than inflicting revenge on that lowlife. *That coward.*

Kyle hurried across the snowfield, the wind and chill finally getting to him. Adrenaline wearing off. Heart settling back to a serene beat.

He opened the door and rumbled down the stairs, placing both bags underneath his and Kennedy's coats. He walked slowly, casually to the bedroom. His face returning to its natural color. She was still there on the bed with Shadow beside her, perking his ears up. "Hey," he said. That was all he could say. "Uh, you're going to stay here for a while, okay?"

She nodded her head. She knew better than to argue with him over this. Not now. Probably not ever. "It's not a problem?"

He walked into the room from the doorway and sat down behind her. He wrapped his arms around her waist and hugged her. "Of course not." He kissed her cheek. "For you, nothing is ever a bother." That was the truth. He'd go to hell and back again for her.

Her tears had subsided now, her voice calm and strong as if nothing had ever happened. And nothing *would* ever happen again.

"You know what I could do?" asked Kyle.

"What?" she replied, turning her head around to meet his gaze, not caring that his arms were still around her, his skin gently touching hers.

"I could move some stuff around and make the other room into a bedroom," he whispered. "I want you to stay with me for a while," he confessed. "I would love to have you here. I love you." Those words shocked him. Profound for such a moment. He realized what he had just said, and knew he couldn't take them back.

"I know," she said.

He released her. "You knew?"

"It doesn't take a genius to see it." She smiled. "I do, too," she said. "I've just been waiting for you to say it." She turned her body around and kissed his lips. Once. Twice. Three times. She crawled on top of him.

Shadow leapt off the bed and headed into the kitchen for another bite of his chicken and liver dinner.

Kennedy took off his shirt and tossed it on the bed. She ran her hands from his abdomen to his pectoral muscles, feeling their taut nature.

His eyes were wide with disbelief that this was really happening. Remembering all the good times of their friendship.

*Crossing the line now.*

She took off her shirt. Her bra. White. Laced. Skin on skin.

Kissing his neck. Rummaging to his belt. Unfastening the hook.

*Over the line.*

Reaching down. Grabbing him with such sensual pleasure. Kissing his chest. Whispering in his ear, "I love you, Kyle."

It was time for him to be forceful, he thought. He couldn't let Kennedy do all the work. What was he supposed to do? Lay on the bed? Still? Immobile?

He sat up. Kicked off his pants; his red briefs followed. He kissed her neck as the light disappeared from the rectangle windows that stood just above the rose bush covered with frost and snow outside.

Naked, he kissed her passionately as any two people who were in love did.

*Were they?*

From the nightstand drawer, Kennedy took out a purple package, tore it open, and handed it to Kyle. And as he fitted the condom, Kennedy took off her pants; white trim-cut underwear fell to the ground.

Sitting on top of Kyle, she couldn't help but notice how attractive he was. A good physique. Eyes for wonderment. And as two bodies, they became one.

Her touch was gentle. Kind. Sweeter than any other feeling he had ever felt before. All at once, his memories of the day were vanquished. The nightmare. Gone. The harsh memory of dealing with her father. Gone. All he felt was her heart thumping with such passion. Tiny gasps of breath escaped her erratically as Kyle began thrusting more fervently.

With the clouds hiding the sun, gray gloom fell into the bedroom. Almost darkness. Kyle was inside her, pushing in with a gentle ease. Loving her like he never had the courage to before; feeling her for the first time like a blind man. Her breasts were elegant and firm. Smooth. Feeling her nipples. Gazing into her eyes. And when he could hold himself no longer, he cried blissfully. Kennedy sang, too. Both collapsed in a breathy stillness. Naked to the world around them. The safest place both of them could be: with each other.

It may have not been the right thing to do, Kyle thought solemnly, but he loved her. He cared about her. He was going to be with her.

*Joseph McGee*

# III

January 20th, 2009. 5:19P.M

    Jack sat at his desk in the crowded station. Phones were ringing; actors in a crime were giving officers a hard time. It was common ground for a Friday evening. By now, Rebecca and Jack should have gone home, taking some notes with them to read over. But today was different; both were staying a few hours late. There were files that needed to be read; the medical examiner had sent over paperwork on Craig Long and last Tuesday's victim, Mark Buffels.

    Comparing, the two were like apples and oranges. No distinctive pattern. No similarities whatsoever, except they were both members of the Snow Hill Country Club.

    The bartender there was now placed as a main suspect, and after Jack and Rebecca couldn't find him at his home, an APB was issued on him for questioning on the two recent deaths. The one thing neither Jack nor Rebecca could put together were the handprints that were burnt in by some wood-burning tool. They couldn't place an exact model on the craft. All that was left for evidence was the crust ridge of the prints. They were exactly five inches long by three inches wide, and they were made with an extra fine point and were very detailed, as if there *was* an infant with the supernatural power to burn on touch.

    When Jack went to work, his emotions were buried so deep within himself that they couldn't be found. It was the only way to work the job, he believed. Coming in with too much anger or too much happiness could break a cop.

    *Those prints could symbolize something*, Jack thought to

himself. *He's a bartender. He serves patrons of the club. He's a servant. The handprints could symbolize serving someone.* There could be a dozen possibilities for this. That's what cops did; made up a lot of different scenarios to be played out. Go over it again and again. Eliminate the less likely to the more probable. Match a profile to the killer and arrest him with good police work. Jack wanted to get this *sicko* before a third victim arose.

Unlike some serials that Jack had researched (Manson, Bundy, etc.), this guy didn't seem to take any type of trophy or memorabilia from his victims. Everything seemed intact, except for the stomach of Mr. Craig Long, where the cause of death was deep lacerations to the abdomen. *There's got to be something I'm missing.*

Jack sat back in his chair, staring thoughtfully at the ceiling, trying to mute the audible surroundings. While immune to his own collective thoughts, Jack took notice of the throng of criminals that had arrived within the past two hours. Domestic squabbles. Vandalism. Druggies. DUIs.

Rebecca came up behind Jack, startling him and breaking his concentration. "Here's your coffee." She sat the foam cup down on his newly organized desktop.

"Thanks," he smiled, then took a long sip of the morning-old drink.

"Looking over the reports?"

"Yeah." He stared at his desk blankly.

"What's wrong?"

"Nothing," he said gloomily. "I'll be happy when this one's over." Jack shuffled through more papers, eyeing them carefully, making sure no detail went overlooked. Just a few minutes before, he had given a call to the Tuesday victim's brother, who resided in Connecticut. There was no answer, so he left a message on the machine asking for a call back to discuss his brother's death further and reiterating the questions once more. Jack wanted to see if there was another incident involving the bartender that had gone unmentioned.

It was already turning into a long day for both of them, and they were on overtime right now, plus a lunch break that neither of them took.

Jack looked at Rebecca, catching her attention and mouthing the words, "I love you." She winked and nodded her head. She loved him, too.

Pushing the papers to the side again, Jack glanced at the clock. It was nearing five-thirty and he was starving. The snow outside had come down mightily, but had long stopped and the streets had been plowed. He wondered if Rebecca would want to go out or stay in tonight. Either would suit him fine. Any chance to get out of the station, relax, and enjoy a good meal.

Looking at the photos of the crime scene was a hard task. Anyone with a weak stomach or a faint heart couldn't do it. Jack had to put the pieces together, but somehow it seemed like a puzzle where the pieces were just too big to fit.

Not many similarities could be made between the two deceased. They were both male. They both belonged to the Snow Hill Country Club, but had been members at different times. Back to square one.

Jack eyed the pictures of Craig Long's stomach, busting out with organs, looking like some jack-in-the-box gone horribly wrong. It takes a strong person to look at that, and an even stronger stomach to tolerate such grotesque images.

A tall and slender black man approached Jack. "Jack," the man said, "we got another homicide. A quadruple, we believe."

Jack looked up from the pictures. "Handprint?"

"Yeah. Four sets."

"Who's on the scene, Lieutenant?" asked Rebecca.

"A half-dozen black and whites," he said calmly, as if this was an ordinary thing to happen. His eyes were glary from stress, his body sluggish from overwork.

As far back as Jack could recall, there had never been a quadruple homicide in Snow Hill. This bastard was sick. Demented. Someone you need to lock up in the crazy house and throw away the key.

The Lieutenant took a small square paper from his caramel overcoat and handed it to Jack. "Got a couple witnesses on this one. Run out and take a look. I want to nail this bastard." He gave a sympathetic smile, as if to say, "I wish I could go home, too, Jack."

Jack got up from his desk, took one last sip of coffee, then swung his coat on from its folded position on the back of his chair; Rebecca did the same. "What about OT?"

"I'll clear it with the captain," Lieutenant Harris said.

Jack looked at the paper. It read: 302 SOUTH MAPLE, APT. # 2.

"Stay there for a little while, then go home," Harris said. "I'll get a couple of the night detectives to work on it 'til morning."

"Thanks, Lieu," said Jack.

Harris nodded and went back to his office which sat off to the left of the station floor. Blinds shut. Door closed. He didn't want to be disturbed. He was going on ten hours and the day was dragging by, plus the snow storm brought a promise that he would have to dig out the driveway and the front steps when he got home. Unless some neighborhood kid wanted to earn some extra cash. He'd gladly give over twenty bucks if it would save a throbbing back in the morning.

Rebecca and Jack headed for the parking garage. Jack still had the keys. He once again took the liberty of driving in the snow- and ice-infested streets.

The night had gotten even colder, blowing something fierce and chilled at the bodies of the innocents who desperately longed for their heated homes. Still, this wasn't anything compared to the snow storm that had been called for the weekend. Jack suddenly realized that he might have to come in Saturday morning. *Didn't Lieutenant Harris say something about tomorrow morning? Let me and Becca finish it up? Damnit. I need a vacation before I erode.* His thoughts lingered in his head, screaming to get out. Earlier today, he had no intention of coming in tomorrow or the next couple days he was supposed to be off during the week. *But criminals don't take days off.* It was a damned if you do, damned if you don't sort of thing.

Before he got in the driver's seat, he popped the trunk and took out a few pairs of latex gloves for this scene in case the occasion required it, and more than likely than not it would. The car started up on the second try and Jack allowed ten minutes to heat the interior.

South Maple Avenue was a good distance away. An average drive of a half-hour in good weather. The streets, as Jack expected, were coated in a shiny glare of snow and ice, hard and compacted by snowplows and other types of vehicles. It left a field of brilliant sparkles.

While driving, Jack asked, "Do you think this could be some sort of satanic ritual?"

"I doubt it," Rebecca said, smoothing out her coat from the fastened seatbelt. "There's no satanistic hallmark ... unless those handprints had something to do with some freaked-out religious cult."

"I went to Sunday school," Jack replied, "and I never heard anything about small handprints burnt into something."

"Well, there you go," Rebecca said reassuringly. "If you really want, we can contact the Boston boys and see if they could lend us a Special Crime Unit for the week. See if it is some sort of cult."

"Might as well," Jack said.

Jack pulled up on South Maple and followed it down to where he saw cyan flickers off the surrounding houses. Only two cars had their overheads on. They were both parked across the street. Jack could see three more had pulled up along the curb near the houses wherever they could find room.

Jack didn't bother to turn on his flashers. He parked in back of one of the squad cars that had a vibrant blue strobing from the roof. He turned off the ignition; he and Rebecca exited and walked across the street.

This was a middle-class neighborhood lined with apartment complexes that varied in size and occupants. 302 South Maple was no different. The second and third floors had balcony porches. And on the left was a set of three windows curving around, making no complete angles.

Jack looked at the house and asked Rebecca demurely, "Is this the right place?"

"I guess," she shrugged.

He put his arm around her. Grinned playfully. Looked at her endearingly. Not worried if any fellow cops could see. Around these parts, they protected their own; Jack had no hard conflicts with anyone on the force, nor did Rebecca. Just two cops earning a paycheck.

Up the short steps and on to a full-sized front porch that had a snow-covered rocking chair at one end of it. The front door was unlocked and ajar. He remembered the piece of paper had read 'apartment two' and he started to climb the carousal stairs, winding up to the second floor platform of henna carpeting filled with dirt and wet swatches of footprints.

The door was shut. The entire building looked dead. Unoccupied. No audible noises escaped from any of the apartments. Rebecca knocked on the door twice. A young man opened it. Disgust and horror lined his face, as if he were about to vomit on the already grungy carpet.

Jack knew. He'd seen that look before. He took the kid by his arm and walked him down the carpeted steps to get some fresh air; something that would do him good. No sooner did they step out onto the porch but the man vomited over the side in a hazel liquid, chunks of not yet digested food spewing from his mouth; nostrils flaring from the vile stench.

"You okay, kid?" asked Jack, waiting for the young man to have one last stomach pump over the railing, caking the perfect white snow into a yellow unpleasantness.

He looked up at Jack, mucus dripping from the corners of his mouth. "I'm so sorry about that," he said, embarrassed. "That's never happened before."

*He was a young kid. First few months probably. It happens.*

"What's your name?"

He coughed and wiped the mucus away from his mouth and onto his navy blue work pants. "Scott. Scott Nestles."

"You going to be all right if I go upstairs?" Jack was trying hard not to laugh.

He nodded his head, yes. "I think I'll stay out here for a bit. I'm so sorry, sir."

"It happens," Jack smiled and went back inside to find Rebecca.

She was standing next to Greg Davis, an overzealous jokester who never took his job seriously a day in his life … until today.

Jack had never seen his face so blank of expression; jaw taut, eyes grimacing in pure horror. When Rebecca spun around, locking gazes with him, it made Jack feel like a little child afraid of the closet-monsters. She reminded him of good ole Scott, yakking his guts out over the railing of the porch. He stood in authentic befuddlement, wanting to ask her what she had seen, but her expression was convincing of it enough. Something horrible. Evil. Making her look so pale and weak.

53

He heard muffled chatter from somewhere in the apartment.

Greg threw a look up at Jack. "This is some sick shit," he said.

He broke his silence and asked Rebecca, "What is it?"

It took her a moment to respond. She had to let the imagery sink in, that this was really happening and not some false hallucination produced by some very large amounts of alcohol, although a tall glass of anything right now might blur her memory with a temporary fix. "I've never used this term on any paperwork I've ever filed before," she said. "Flayed."

Jack had to wait a minute for the definition to sink in before he got the urge to look into the door that had Greg Davie still staring. He was not moving his eyes, like it hypnotized him to stare at some god-awful monstrosity.

Jack crept closer, peering through the door. In the bathtub lay a river of blood. It was caked like a stream of tears overflowing the tub sitting at the far end. It splattered the walls and toilet and sink. There were four sets of legs and only three complete sets of arms; the fourth victim was missing what appeared to be a left arm. All the remaining legs and arms had been skinned; muscle and tissue seemed to be the only thing left on them.

On the cobalt-tiled wall, burned in place, were four handprints. One per victim. A stench formed from something that Jack never had the distasteful pleasure of smelling before.

Jack turned his face away from the door, revulsion plain on his brow. "What the hell happened here?"

Greg walked closer to Jack as if to whisper the story in his ear, but to keep it quiet from the neighbors who could be peeping or listening with nosy ears. "We first got a call from an elderly woman downstairs about a loud noise that she was shaking her ceiling. Nobody rushed over here to tell them to turn down the TV." Greg said, sounding more professional than ever. "Ten minutes goes by and a second complaint comes in from a couple on the third floor. They were eavesdropping by the door and said they could hear men begging for their lives. Screaming in pain. They dialed 911 and we got here in five minutes." His freshly shaved face gave him a new look, a more desirable appearance that made him look like a good cop instead of an idiot thriving on making jokes at others' expense rather than his own. "The rest of the guys are sweeping around, looking for evidence or signs of what the hell happened."

"Forced entry?"

"Doesn't appear to be. Door was unlocked when we got here."

"Thanks," Jack said. "Let me call this in." Jack, from his inside coat pocket, took a cell phone out and speed dialed the Lieutenant. In three rings, he answered in a rough, weary voice. "It's Jack," he said. "We need a clean-up crew here, pronto."

"What's going on?" asked Harris.

"We got four dead people here in a bathtub full of blood and guts. They look as if they've been skinned."

"I'll send forensics and cleanup there now," Harris said. "Jack, I want to catch this fucker."

"Me, too."

"Why don't you head home now. Take the unmarked with you and head back tomorrow morning. There's not a whole lot you can do until it's patted down for evidence.

"Yeah," Jack agreed willingly. "See you in the A.M." He hung up the phone.

Rebecca still looked nauseous, and the best thing he could do was take her home and get her in bed for a good night's rest. Maybe a shower beforehand. Something to wash this horrible nightmare from her mind. He looked at her. She was gasping. Panting with nervousness—and anxiety.

"Greg, we're heading out. The Lieutenant is sending over another team to clean up," Jack explained. "Make sure any findings get back to us."

"You got it, Jack," he agreed with a thin smile. "Have a good night."

Jack walked Rebecca outside. She could walk, but her eyes had the image of the scene stamped into them and all she could see was death; flayed bodies lying in a bathtub with overflowing blood dribbling down the side of it in a motion of ghastly waves crashing over the porcelain edge, staining everything a dark crimson. Tainting her sane mind.

Scott was off the porch now and back in his cruiser with the window halfway down. That was enough heat to warm his body, and the right amount of fresh air to give him the slight hope that he wouldn't vomit in his car. The lieutenant would hate that.

"We're going home now, okay?"

Rebecca nodded, more or less unaware of what she had agreed to, until a chilly wind broke her hold. "We're going home?" she asked, not remembering completely what Jack had just said.

"Yeah. A nice bath and some—" No. He couldn't mention food. She'd barf for sure and color more snow, the same way Scott Nestles had earlier. No. A nice bath and bed. If she was hungry, fine. But the look on her face gave a guarantee that she wouldn't be eating tonight.

Jack helped Rebecca climb in the car, although she could manage it herself. If she asked why, he could use the simple answer that he was being a gentleman and getting the door for his lady. That wouldn't have worked, though, but it was something to say to hide the truth that he was worried about her. Fortunately, no explanation was necessary.

Jack ran across to his side, escaping from the night's dank

air, and turned over the ignition, finding pleasure in the car's heat.

In the radiant light of blue flickers bouncing off her skin, Rebecca looked almost like her normal self. Her color had come back and she seemed more aware.

Jack shifted the car into reverse, pulling away from the back bumper of Scott's cruiser, then drove down the street. Heading for home.

*Joseph McGee*

# IV

January 20th, 2009. 7:45P.M

Kyle lay in his bed, covers half on him, staring at the ceiling in utter contentment. Kennedy's head lay on his chest, the blankets pulled up to her breasts until she threw them off of herself, climbed over Kyle, and began getting dressed.

Kyle was watching her thoughtfully, thinking to himself, *God, she's beautiful* before he, too, had to get from dressed, in hopes of preparing the dinner that he had promised before it got any later. He looked at the alarm clock on the nightstand beside his bed. In neon-green it read 7:47 P.M. He wanted to be done with dinner an hour ago, but other things had caught his attention. Other things like Kennedy.

Kyle threw his clothes back on and started boiling the water on the stove, and in a much smaller pan, began heating some sauce on the back burner.

They finished eating just before eight-thirty. Kyle cleared the table, placed both plates in the sink, and ran hot water on them to wash away the sauce that still remained.

From the living room couch where Kennedy sat and Shadow lay with his head on her lap, she called, "Have you ever thought about the future and getting married and stuff?"

Like some sort of punch line in a sitcom, Kyle coughed as if he were choking on some loose meat not fully chewed. "Marriage? What?"

"Relax," she said, "I wasn't proposing." She laughed a little at the embarrassed smirk on Kyle's face. "I was just asking."

Maybe it wasn't such a bad idea. Perhaps he could give

her the ring his grandmother had left before she passed away eight years ago. His dad still had it in the floor safe in the back of the walk-in closet in his parents' bedroom, hidden behind some boxes filled with old relics of their youth back. His dad often thought about putting in a wall safe behind a painting of some sort but that plan went to hell when he hadn't the money or the "okay" from his wife to do so.

It was still early in their relationship. What relationship? They'd had sex once, followed by dinner. Was this even considered a date? If so, was marriage to follow? No. That wasn't Kyle's idea, nor did he have any idea what exactly Kennedy meant by asking him such a complex and quarrelsome question.

The whole topic temporarily dropped, Kyle found himself standing by the television, looking over the shelves around it for a movie to pop in. *Comedy? Action? Romance?* It had to be one of those three. It wouldn't quite hit the mood if he threw in a horror flick from the George Romero era.

After the movie, they spent time talking over a gallon of ice cream and two spoons. Double Chocolate Chip Chunk. Kyle's favorite, and he believed it was Kennedy's, too.

It was getting late. Kyle looked at Kennedy thoughtfully, licking each scoop of the ice cream with some pleasure. *What if I went upstairs and got that ring? It would look good on her.* Too soon. It was nearing eleven o'clock. His parents were probably sound asleep. Then there was that heavy blizzard. He wanted to see the news before he went to bed, but he found gratification in not knowing. He already knew that it would last at least the entire weekend and then some. Snowed in for hours, if not days. A cold chill frosting up the windows, as if it were that perfect Christmas evening. He would turn the heat on to seventy-five tonight to make sure that it would be warm enough in the morning. Kyle always found that it was much colder in the wee hours of the morning than in the late of night.

Kyle took a much-needed, refreshing shower before getting ready for bed. Although images of Kennedy sneaking in to join him played through his mind, in fact she waited until he was done to shower herself. Then she brushed her teeth and slipped into a faded old t-shirt that was a size or two too big for her.

Kyle lay beside her on the right side of the bed, closest to the door. The windows that stood above the bed and just barely above the ground on the outside were now blocked by a white barricade of snow. Not much was supposed to fall tonight, but tomorrow.... Saturday was going to be a god-awful storm.

Within minutes, both of them had fallen asleep. Kyle dreamed.

*Instead of the lava, now it was snow. Thick and packed tightly. He stood centered in the middle of nowhere. No one was around him; nothing was around him. He was knee deep in it. Trying to kick his legs through it and move. Walk somewhere. There was nowhere to walk to. No buildings or houses or cars, just an emptiness like Antarctica. Just as cold and featureless, too. Then it came into view. The same vision as in his other dream. He saw them again. Now there were even more people. They sat isolated on a land far from him. They were screaming for him. Yelling for him to hurry before it was too late. His legs couldn't move fast enough.*

*Kennedy reaching out for him.*

*Him yelling, "I'm coming."*

*Falling to his knees, using his hands to paddle through the snow like he was swimming in the great blue ocean. Snow seeping through his jeans and shirt didn't protect him much against the bitter wind or the frigidness of the snow.*

*He was beleaguered. The snow had come down with such a mighty force that seemed to only push away from where Kennedy stood. The others were waiving him on.*

*"Snow Hill is dead," one of the isolated ones said.*

*Everyone but Kennedy looked like shadows to him. Dancing silhouettes in an immense flame.*

*The day sky turning to twilight. The remnants of anything in back of Kyle had gone blank and non-existent in an inky-black field that left a promise that he would be next to be non-existent.*

*Struggling. Fighting for his own life.*

*Being sucked in by the darkness. His hand reaching out for help, then disappearing behind a wall of blackness and gloom.*

Kyle woke up in a silent hesitation. He lay there, looking all around the room, as if he expected someone other than Kennedy to be there. His body was a cold mess. Freezing. His toes becoming numb; his nipples painfully erect.

Kyle had decided to only wear a pair of silk boxers to bed and nothing else. He climbed out from under the covers, careful not to wake Kennedy. He pulled a shirt and pea-colored sweatpants out of his dresser drawer, put them on, and slid back into bed unnoticed by Kennedy or Shadow, who had migrated somewhere else. Moments later, Kyle drifted off to an easier, more peaceful sleep.

* * *

In the wee hours of the morning, Jack found himself sitting alone at the kitchen table with the light on over the kitchen sink that gave off a glow like soft butter melting over the kitchen until it turned into shadows at the far end near the living room and by the stairs; organized piles of papers covered most of the table. He went over the paperwork from the previous night while Rebecca slept peacefully upstairs.

Jack had received a phone call from Hugh Willmon earlier that night. The bite marks on Craig Long's face were categorized as "unknown." It was some type of reptile, Hugh said, or something like it, but there was no exact match, except for the structure the tooth left behind. That neon green goop that slithered out of his face was also "unknown." The material was not listed on any of the charts. Hugh had told him that he'd never seen such a thing before and there was nothing to go on. That left Jack struggling over these photos and reports with tired eyes.

It was nearing two A.M. and Jack noticed a light flurry from outside the window over the sink. A fine sheet had covered the streets more completely, leaving a pure white blanket beneath the city lights. Only an inch or two rested on the ground, but the plows were beginning to come out. All those city workers getting paid twenty-something an hour to drive up and down the street.

*What the fuck is going on?* Jack thought intently to himself, eyeing the papers more carefully, trying rigorously to pinpoint some pattern between the murders. He hadn't collected any of the reports from the most recent killings. He'd collect those tomorrow when he had to go in. Jack wanted to make Rebecca stay home and take a nice bubble bath with candles all around the tub or whatever it was that she liked to do to relax after seeing people torn up and bashed together in some evil pool of themselves. But he knew she wouldn't stay put.

As he finished off the last sip of his coffee, placed the mug in the sink, and ran water on it from the faucet, his eyes caught the glare of the headlights on a city plow, scraping the streets and pushing the already built-up snow further into people's driveways.

\* \* \*

Morning came rather quickly, and Jack had only gotten the few winks of sleep that the downstairs couch had allowed. The sun behind the clouds illuminated the city in a pure grayness. Snow had fallen not too long before, and picked up mass just a while ago, coating the streets another foot or more, enticing plows to scrape the city roads once more.

Rebecca walked down the stairs in a pink cotton robe with sleep-matted eyes. Her skin pale; her face blank of expression. She got a mug of coffee and took a warm sip, letting it linger on her tongue before she swallowed.

In all Jack's years, he'd never seen her like this. He wanted to comfort her, to stay home with her today, but their job needed to get done. He had no choice in that matter. This murderous bastard wasn't going to get away with killing nearly a half-dozen people in such a way that made Bundy look like a saint.

He kept thinking about what animal could do something like this. Obviously what killed them was human, but what kind of animal could have done something like this? And what kind of sick bastard could have done that to those poor men in the bathtub? Someone without a conscious. Someone without feeling. He couldn't help but wonder if there would be any more victims, if any other poor soul would be next on this "hit list."

\* \* \*

Martinez walked up to the desk with a small stack of files in his hand, "Jack, I checked on those divorce cases from the second victim. All clean. No criminal record on anyone."

"Good job. Thanks," Jack said.

Martinez was the youngest guy on the detective squad, but so far he had been proving himself to be a valued asset. He was a quick thinker, and he had Roberts as his partner.

Roberts was the eldest on the squad. The most experienced out there. He was pushing fifty and had thirty years of service on the force.

Jack waited for Rebecca to return from the coffee room.

She had gone to get some soft drinks from the vending machine for herself and Jack.

Jack finished writing up reports for the second victim, and he still had more reports to work on. He contemplated whether or not to take the paperwork home with him and finish it there. He always felt that being a cop, whether it be a rookie or someone with forty years on the job, was a full-time thing. It didn't matter if you punched in or not. When you got your badge, it was a lifetime commitment.

"Jack," Harrison said from his office, "come here for a minute."

Jack got up from his desk and walked over to the corner office. "What's up, boss?"

"Dispatch got another call," Harrison explained. "This woman called 9-1-1 just a few minutes ago. She's calling about another murder. It's one of her neighbors, Joshua and Sarah McClain. She somehow saw the handprints. She's afraid that the killer might be after her next. She claims that the killer was black and about eight feet tall with small hands and a tail."

"A tail?"

"Probably a nut case, but check it out anyway. The woman's name is Martha Clarks."

"You got it," Jack said. "Mind if I take a couple of the night-tour guys with us?"

"Sure," Harrison agreed. "It's at 118 Harrington."

Jack left the office and walked back to his desk. Rebecca was sitting down at her own desk, which faced his, sipping on her cola and rummaging through some loose papers.

"You should get some organizers, Becca," Jack teased. "We got another call. From a neighbor, claims to have seen the handprints."

"All right, let's go," she said.

"I want to take Bryant and Michaels."

Jack went to Bryant's desk. "Listen, we got a serial on our hands," Jack explained. "I don't know if you've been told that or not, but I want you guys with me. This is the fourth killing this week. We got a witness. A neighbor. Not sure how helpful she's going to be."

"Sure, Jack," Ken Michaels said, "we'll tag along."

Michaels and Bryant stopped what they were doing, picked their coats up from the coat rack standing at the doorway, headed for the parking garage, and left for the crime scene in their car.

# V

January 21st, 2009. 05:17p.m.

"You want to go pick up some of your clothes?" Kyle asked.

"Yeah," she said. "Before the storm gets any worse."

There was a nice, gentle fire going in the fireplace that Kyle and his dad had put in over the summer, on the side wall of the living room opposite the couch. He had a screen up in front of it. He always feared that Shadow might get to close to it and catch his tail on fire. Even though he knew Shadow was smart enough not to do that, he was prepared nonetheless. He had two fire extinguishers mounted on either side of the sofa; plus one in the bedroom and a couple underneath the kitchen sink.

"I told you," she said, "nothing good is on."

"Well, if you want we can order a dirty movie."

She laughed, "Oh yeah. Such entertainment."

"Or we can make one of our own," he told her.

She laughed again, "Shut up, you!"

"C'mon, let's go get some of your clothes," Kyle said.

He helped Kennedy up off the comfortable couch and followed her to get their jackets off the coat hooks.

Kyle slipped on his jacket and then pulled on a white ski mask he'd picked up a few weeks before. It snuggled around his face, gently keeping his head warm. The only holes were a wide patch around the eyes and another one around the mouth.

Kennedy zippered her coat and unraveled the collar to protect her neck from the bursts of wind and snow.

"You ready?"

"As ever," she said.

Kennedy pushed open the heavy oak door. The wind came rushing in, almost knocking her back down the stairs.

The snow was heavy and the wind whistled through the bare trees in the yard. It was one of the coldest days that season. Anything more than five or six feet away was invisible. They kept their heads down, both to avoid the snow in their faces and to watch their footing in the ankle-deep snow. They fought their way through the snow and wind until they finally met the back stairs.

The steps were growing ice on them, and the snow on top of that made it even slicker on the wooden stairs.

They went up the stairs, grabbing the railing tightly to hold their balance steady. When they reached the top platform, Kyle's house couldn't be seen, nor anything else, except one pine tree to the right.

Kennedy banged her feet on the doorjamb so as to not track too much snow in the house; Kyle did the same and shut the door behind them.

The house was warm with the sweet fragrance of recently cooked food. Pans still sat in the sink waiting to be washed clean.

"I wonder where they are," Kennedy whispered.

"It don't matter," he told her. "Let's just get your stuff and head back."

"My dad is probably at the stupid club."

"What club?"

"He joined the Snow Hill Country Club a couple of months ago," she said. "He usually gets drunk there."

"Your mom goes with him?"

"Not often," she said, "but she has."

"Do you really think they would have gone out in the blizzard?"

"Anything is possible," she said.

They walked past the kitchen table into the hall where Kyle had met her father and continued down to the last door on the right. Kennedy's bedroom.

Kennedy didn't waste time. She opened the closet door and took out three large duffel bags before she took the hanging clothes and threw them on the bed.

She didn't bother to fold the clothes before she forced them into the first bag, zipped it shut, and placed it down at the doorway.

"What are you taking?"

"Everything I'm going to need," she said. "I don't want to come back here again."

Kyle stood still and examined her room closely.

He had been in her room before, but it had been a while ago. If either of them were to spend time together, it was usually at Kyle's place or somewhere else, but never there. Never in that house. It was her family, and she would love them for that fact, but she hated being there.

Kennedy went over to her dresser and emptied all the drawers with makeup and underwear and shirts and pants and anything else that was there while Kyle held the bright-red bag opened; she filled it before she got to the bottom drawer.

Kyle gathered a couple dozen CDs that sat next to her stereo, which he didn't bother taking because he already had two of them at his place, and it just wouldn't fit anywhere. They didn't bother taking the twenty-inch television, either.

Kennedy tossed a couple of stuffed animals in one of the bags and headed to the bathroom to get her hair care products to put them in as well. By the time she retuned Kyle had put everything in the bags that could fit. He loaded his jacket pockets with some miscellaneous things to conserve space, but everything she wanted to take was packed.

The room looked bare. There had been no decorations on

the walls to begin with, just a soft pink paint with a floral border. Only one dresser sat to the side of the window, and a twin bed sat in the middle. Her desk was next to the closet door, and next to it was a small table she used to hold the T.V.

"We got everything?"

"Just one more thing," she said. Kennedy went in the closet and pulled something off one of the shelves. "Got it."

She came down with a small fireproof safe.

"What in there?" Kyle asked.

"A lot of money."

She stared at her room, looking at it blankly. Thinking to herself that she was now free.

"Give me the safe," Kyle said.

"It's a little heavy," she warned him.

Kyle took one of the duffel bags on one shoulder and carried the heavy safe in his left hand.

"Can you get the other two?"

"Yeah." Kennedy lifted up the bags, flipped the lights off, and walked out of the room.

"What's this?" she asked. She dropped down the bags at the end of the hall, just before the kitchen.

"What's what?"

Kennedy ran her fingers across some etchings burned into the wall. They were maybe three or four inches across and looked like little tiny hands and little tiny fingers. "Forget about it," he told her. "This stuff weighs a ton."

She picked up her bags and stayed quiet so as to not alert anyone, if anyone was home.

Kyle turned the brass doorknob and the cold wind whipped in. The tree branches were shaking back and forth. The night's sky stayed lit with the white flakes of snow still making their way down to Earth. Maybe it would calm down and be a light dusting later tonight, but Kyle doubted it. He didn't care too much. He loved the snow, even though he had to help his dad shovel it and to use the snow blower in the driveway and walkways. It was magical to him for some strange reason. He liked the idea of being snowed in. Light the fireplace up, have a cup of hot chocolate, watch some movies and watch the snow pile up outside the windows; but by now, the windows were already covered up, just like his truck was.

Kyle cursed his way through the snow. His dungarees were getting soaked with the moisture of the slushy snow and then turning into shards of ice at his ankles.

"This sucks," Kennedy yelled above the wind.

"Oh, where's your winter spirit?"

"Freezing its ass off," she said.

Kyle laughed as he opened the door and let Kennedy go in first down the stairs.

He thought about just tossing the bags of stuff down after her, but it wasn't his stuff to be tossing. Kyle bore with the weight and walked down the steps, trying not to slip from the snow and ice stuck to the ends of his boots. He was barely able to close the door behind him.

He placed the bag at the bottom of the steps and sat the safe on top of the kitchen table.

Shadow ran up and rubbed against Kennedy, then Kyle. Happy once again for their return as he was every time. It didn't matter if Kyle was gone for a minute or gone for days, that dog would act as if he hadn't seen him in years.

"Safe's on the table," Kyle said.

"Okay, let me show you what's in it."

Kennedy pulled a ring of keys out of her pocket, fumbled to find the right one, and unlocked the safe.

It was filled with money. Top to bottom. All fifty dollar bills and a couple dozen rolls of change.

"There's a little over eleven-thousand dollars," she told

him.

"Where did you get that kind of money?"

"It's college money," she said. "My parents have been giving me fifty bucks a week since I turned twelve, and the change is from me. There would be more, but I used it to buy the laptop and some clothes."

"That's good," he said. "At least they gave you something."

She didn't say anything.

"Next time we go to the bank we can open a bank account for you."

"All right."

Kennedy locked up the safe and Kyle put it on the floor of the bedroom closet.

Kyle took off his jacket and helped Kennedy with hers. He hung them back up by the door. He was anxious to get his pants off; his legs were cold and a little wet from the melted snow. He unbuckled his belt and unbuttoned his jeans, then sat down on the kitchen chair and removed his boots one-by-one. He took off his fleece socks, stuffed them inside his empty boots, and went to the bedroom to change into something more comfortable.

Kennedy walked in on him as he took off his pants, but he didn't try to cover up as he might have a couple of days earlier.

"I just wanted to put these in here," she said, putting the bags of clothes down by the queen-size bed.

"I know what you really wanted."

"Oh, yeah. You stud muffin, you," she laughed.

Kyle kicked off his jeans, put on a pair of flannel pajama pants his parents had gotten him for Christmas, and threw on a plain tank top. His house-wear clothes, he called them. Something to just kick back in.

He didn't know what to do next. It was snowing. Strong. He couldn't go out anywhere; the roads wouldn't be drivable.

And he would assume that a lot of the businesses had to be closed, or would be closing soon. The snow was just too bad. The only people who would be let on the road would be emergency response vehicles. Kyle wasn't going to try to go somewhere and get stuck out on the road.

He finally lay down on the sofa, and Kennedy joined him a few minutes later. She had on a pair of Kyle's boxers and a big shirt.

She lay in between his legs with her head on his chest and Shadow at their feet.

The news came on and issued a weather emergency telling people not to leave their homes and if there was an emergency to dial 9-1-1.

But he wasn't going out. He was sitting across from a roaring fire, holding his girl in his arms. Nothing could drag him away from this. Nothing.

\* \* \*

Jack finally got Martha Clarks to calm down after a couple of cups of tea.

"You have to understand, Miss Clarks," Jack said, "you're describing a giant monkey with a long pointy tail."

"That's what I saw," she said. "The thing was hideous. I only saw it for a minute, but I got a good look at it."

"Okay," Rebecca said, "why don't you give us the description one more time to make sure it's accurate."

"Very tall. Eight feet or so. It was black. Not like a black man," she said, "but the skin was pitch-black. A long snout for his head. I couldn't really see its eyes. I don't even know if it had any. It had these two small hands, like some kind of defect on it. It had claws on its feet and the tail was almost as tall as the body and it had a spear on the end of it. A really sharp one."

"All right," Jack said. "Thank you for your help ma'am."

Jack walked away, took out his cell phone, and called the squad room."

"Harrison," the Lieutenant picked up.

"Lieutenant, it's Jack."

"What do you got for me?"

"I'm not sure whether to put an A.P.B. out for a deformed monkey, an alien, or Bigfoot."

"That bad, huh?"

"Oh, yeah."

"What did crime scene pick up?"

"Nothing," Jack said. "Just the handprints and some bright green goop."

"What is it?"

"They don't know yet, but they're leaving in a few minutes to take it back to the lab."

"I want to know what it is as soon as they do," Harrison said.

"Yes, sir."

"Where's Michaels and Bryant?"

"I sent them back," Jack said. There was nothing for them to do over here but watch the crime scene."

"All right, inform me when you have something."

Jack hung up the phone and placed it back in his pocket.

He viewed the apartment, looking for something out of the ordinary, but couldn't find anything out of place. Not a single thing. The apartment was very clean and very orderly.

He returned to the elderly woman, now sitting on her rocking chair instead of her floral-patterned couch.

"What if that thing comes back for me?"

"Do you have family to go to?" Rebecca asked.

"I could stay with my daughter," she said.

"Good," Rebecca nodded. "Stay there."

Jack walked out the apartment and into the grungy hallway.

An officer was standing outside the door, guarding it from the neighbors who had gathered around to the see what the commotion was about.

Most of them were talking amongst themselves. Rumors would probably fly through their families about how a murder had happened right next door to them.

"Back these people up," Jack said to the young cop, "we got a crime scene here."

Another cop that was already in the apartment came out to help the other officer bar off the neighbors.

Jack went back to the crime scene. Hugh Brown was kneeling next to the latest victim, Andrew Keene.

"Got the cause of death yet?"

"My guess," Hugh said, "is something large and heavy through the chest."

"A knife?"

"More along the lines of a wide sword," he said. "You can tell by the tear in the skin."

"How wide would this sword have to be?"

"Well the cut is fourteen inches."

"How do you know that it wasn't just a pocket knife and he just cut across?"

"For one, it exited the other side," Hugh explained. "And see over here," he pointed to the bloody wound through the now-red shirt, "the flesh is ripped and not sliced." He reached for a brown leather wallet on the floor. "This is his."

Jack slapped on a pair of latex gloves and flipped open the wallet.

Eighty-seven dollars in cash and a couple of credit cards, but what stood out to Jack the most was a laminated card. A membership card to the Snow Hill Country Club.

He examined it carefully. It wasn't much more than a regular business card. It had a magnetic strip on the back that would probably let you in the front door, and had the vic's name and address on the front; his member number 0568 was on the right side, underneath his enrollment date of 12/21/2008.

Jack shoved the wallet in his own coat pocket and looked around the apartment some more, checking all the windows carefully again, looking for any sign of an intruder or any sign of forced entry.

Stuck in the blue carpet in the bedroom was more of the greasy goo. Using the edge of the unmade bed to ease his weight down, Jack got on his knees and crawled to his stomach. He took a small flashlight out of his inside coat pocket and pressed it on. Nothing was under the bed; no cell phone and no more of that odious goop.

Jack left the bedroom and checked out the bathroom once more, but everything seemed in place.

A woman's scream got everyone's attention.

A gun shot. Two. Three. Four rounds fired.

Jack ran out the door and back to the neighbor's apartment. He was in last behind the two officers with their guns drawn.

"What is it?" Jack demanded.

Jack took his gun out of his side holster and walked carefully around the woman's apartment.

Rebecca stood in front of Martha Clarks, who was still sitting in her rocking chair.

"Rebecca, what is it?"

"That thing," she said.

"What thing?"

"The thing that she described."

He dropped his tone from seriousness to trivial, "Are you for real?"

"Jack, I saw it," she said. "It was hanging on the wall."

He turned back to one of the uniformed cops, "Call for back-up."

The cop turned away, got on his radio, and requested immediate back up.

"Whatcha names?"

"I'm Tommy," the second cop said and looked over to his partner. "This is Dan."

"All right," Jack said. "We're going to need you guys for this, okay?"

"Becca, where did it go?"

"In the bedroom, I think," she said. "Jack, I hit the thing four times."

Rebecca led the way in front of Jack, followed Tommy and Dan.

The bedroom door had been broken down. Claw marks resided on the walls. Jack knew they hadn't been there before. Maybe something like the old lady described did exist; some kind of wild animal looking for shelter maybe.

Jack flipped on the light and aimed his Glock-17 in front of him, but nothing was there.

There was only a broken window and the snow had started drifting in with a cold, brittle wind.

Once they knew there wasn't a threat, the officers holstered their weapons.

Tommy got back on his radio, "Possible suspect broke out of the window, check the immediate area."

"Thanks guys," Jack said. "Can you give us a minute?"

"Sure," Dan said.

Rebecca waited for the cops to leave. "Jack, I know what I saw."

"I believe you," he said, "but what was it?

"I don't know. It was exactly how she described it. That

thing was just one ugly fuck."

Jack was puzzled. A weird feeling in his gut took over and had to sit down to collect his thoughts. *What kind of animal could it be?* He asked himself over and over again in his head.

Jack was a very open-minded thinker. He believed in all possibilities until a case was solved, but he couldn't believe in monsters or the boogey man.

Jack patted Rebecca on the knee and went out to the hall to examine the marks in the plaster some more.

He lined his right hand up with the marks against the wall, looking each of the indentations. Jack couldn't begin to understand what could have done this. He didn't think Rebecca was lying or exaggerating, but she had been working a lot, and stress can do strange things to you. Something was there. Something had to be. But what? That was the million dollar question.

Jack went back into the bedroom and escorted Rebecca out of the cold room, shutting the door behind them, recalling that Rebecca had said she shot her gun four times, but not finding bullet holes anywhere on the plaster or door.

"I just talked to my daughter, Officers, but she won't be able to come get me until the storm lifts."

"I'll have someone drive you there," Jack offered.

Jack could see that she was shaken up from the gun fire and the intruder. He was worried that she might have a heart attack right in front of them. She had to be in her late sixties, maybe her early seventies, but she was doing fine living by herself. She seemed like a sweet, old lady that would make you chicken noodle soup when you weren't feeling well.

Jack looked Rebecca in the eyes, "Becca, you okay?"

"Yeah," she said, "I'm fine."

"Who are you going to get to drive Miss Clarks to her daughter's?"

"I'll have Tommy and Dan do it," Jack said.

Jack left Rebecca in the apartment and found Tommy waiting by the stairs as the coroner wheeled the body out. "Hey Tommy."

"Yeah Detective?"

"Can you do me a favor and bring Miss Clarks to her daughter's house?"

"Sure, we can do that."

"Thanks," he said.

"Okay," Tommy said. "We taped up the door and Hugh Brown is downstairs about to leave, I think. Me and Dan will be waiting by the front door when she's ready."

Jack walked back down the hall.

The victim's door now had several rows of bright yellow tape that read "POLICE LINE DO NOT CROSS" from side to side.

Jack was contemplating whether or not do go back to the victim's apartment and scrounge around to see if there was anything he had overlooked, but he knew there was nothing else to see. Just like the last one. There was that green stuff that was stuck to the carpet, but it could have been some kind of soft drink or energy drink. Something that could frustrate him even more.

Miss Clarks was ready and waiting in the hall. She had packed a large suitcase with as much clothes as she though she would need for her stay at her daughter's house.

She threw her purse strap over her shoulder. "Officer, I am ready to go."

"Okay, ma'am," Jack said. "Officer …" Jack thought for a little bit and realized he didn't know Tommy's last name. "Officer Tommy is waiting for you downstairs." Jack took the suitcase out of her hand. "Let me take that downstairs for you."

"Oh, thank you very much," she smiled.

Jack walked the suitcase downstairs in front of Miss Clarks, who was taking her time with the stairs.

"Here you go, Tommy," Jack said, handing the suitcase over.

Jack waited for Martha to finish her descent before he went back upstairs.

"Thanks, Tommy," Jack called over his shoulder as he headed back up.

"You owe me and Dan coffee next time," he joked.

"I'll even spring for donuts."

Tommy laughed and shut the door behind Miss Clarks and himself.

"Well, Rebecca," Jack said, "how do you want to write this up?"

"I don't know yet."

"I think I'm getting a hunch again," Jack said. "I think it has something to do with that country club."

"What makes you say that?"

Jack took Andrew Keene's wallet from his coat and carefully pulled out the membership card. "I'm willing to bet, as soon as we ID the other victims, all of them belonged to that same club."

"You think the club is responsible?"

"I'm not sure," Jack said, "but that guy really got under my skin. Just something about him I didn't like."

"We need to head back to the station. It's really bad outside."

"Yeah, it's getting late, too." Jack looked down at his watch, "almost six-thirty."

Rebecca realized that she had been carrying her weapon this whole time. She holstered it. Then she locked the lady's door and pulled it shut behind her.

The wooden floor creaked as Rebecca went down the

stairs; Jack followed behind her.

"Want to drive?"

"No, thanks," Jack said. "It's your turn. I know how much you like to drive in shit-weather like this."

"Oh yeah," she said. "Fun."

"Did you notice anything weird?"

"Like what?"

"The neighbors," Jack said. "Where did they go?"

"I don't know. Probably back into their apartments."

"I didn't hear them," he explained. "I didn't see them."

"They probably heard the gun shots and went back into their apartments," Rebecca said. "Stop being so paranoid."

"Yes, dear."

Rebecca pulled open the front door.

By now, it was nighttime. There was not a single star in the sky, nor was the moon shining down. Nothing but snow, and more snow.

The streets were not visible from the front door. Nothing could be seen. There were no headlights from cars. Nothing. It almost felt like a ghost town. Creepy and rural.

"Let's get back to the station," said Jack as he closed the door and tossed Rebecca the keys.

*Joseph McGee*

# VI

Sitting up in bed with his legs hanging off the side, Jack stared out the window and tried not to wake Rebecca.

She was sleeping so peacefully, tucked underneath the covers, as if she didn't have a care in the world; as if nothing had happened the day before.

He stood still, looking at her sweet expressionless face. But what he was really thinking about was yesterday's events. All of them, especially the four victims from that horrible scene. Only one had been identified thus far. Jacob Stone. It was his apartment, so naturally Stone was one of the victims.

Jack couldn't get that image out of his mind. It's different watching a movie than in real life. No matter how believable the actors may seem, you always know that it's fake. You always know that the victims in a movie will be doing the same thing a few months from now. These four souls would not be coming back. No one should die that way. No one should have to suffer like that, Jack thought.

Wearing nothing but a pair of flannel boxers, Jack got up, put on his slippers, and went to the kitchen to make a cup of coffee.

He looked out the kitchen window. The roads were covered in snow, maybe two or three feet deep. He doubted if he would be able to get to work. His garage door was undoubtedly blocked by a wall of ice and snow. If he wanted to get to the station in a couple of hours, he would have to start shoveling soon to clear a path from his driveway to the street, and maybe by then a plow would come by and push the snow away, or just block the driveway once again.

Jack didn't want to disturb Rebecca in her peaceful slumber. She was exhausted from everything that had happened yesterday, even if Jack didn't completely understand what it was.

Rebecca stayed at Jack's house a lot, even though she had a nice little apartment across town that she rented at eight-hundred dollars a month, plus the standard utilities. They had often discussed moving in with one another. Rebecca would come to live in Jack's house. Everything was all paid for, and it was a nice three-bedroom house.

It had belonged to Jack's parents. After his father died, Jack's sister, Lauren, took their mother down to Florida to live with her and her husband. The house was left to him. Although his sister tried to insist on having Jack pay for at least some of the value, his mother refused to ask for money.

Within the last year or so, Jack had refurbished the entire kitchen and both bathrooms. This year he wanted to try and put in a pool in the backyard for the summer time, and maybe add a Jacuzzi to the mix as well. But that was all in the future. If Rebecca moved in, two pay checks would always be better than one. All his remodeling plans might come into effect sooner than he hoped they would.

* * *

With the snow filtering down, the sun rose just before seven o'clock. Rebecca was just finishing up her shower. Jack was already ready, sitting at the kitchen table eating a couple slices of toast with a light spread of butter on them.

He had started shoveling almost an hour before and barely had anything to show for it, with the exception of an eight-foot-wide path that lasted only two feet.

Jack was going to wait until seven-thirty or so to call in to the station to say he wasn't coming in or he was going to be really late.

He figured the station had to be just as bad, parking garage and all.

Such a massive extent of snow and ice; plus the wind. Jack had never seen a storm like this before in all his life.

He had thought about taking the unmarked and trying to ram the snow bank, but he would surely get stuck. His Mercury was still sitting in the police garage from yesterday.

Rebecca walked out of the bathroom and onto the kitchen's hardwood floor dripping-wet. She wasn't naked; she had a red, cotton robe cloaking her body.

"I hope you made some toast for me," she said.

"It's in the toaster," he said. "Just press it down. I didn't want to make it yet, 'cause I didn't know when you'd be out."

"How's the snow?"

"Well," Jack began, "while you were sleeping I dug us out somewhat. Not a lot." Jack chewed on his last piece of toast. "The damn thing is as tall as me."

Rebecca looked out the second kitchen window in a row of two. "Holy shit," she said. "I didn't think it was that bad out there. We may not be able to get to the station at all."

"I know," Jack said, "and I wanted to go back to the country club, too. See what else we could dig up there."

"Did you call 'em?"

"Not yet, but I'm about to."

"Think the morning paper came?"

"If it did, I would love to see you go look for it."

She laughed. "Go call the station."

"Yes ma'am," Jack retorted. He picked up the phone and called the station.

*Ring. Ring. Ring.*

No answer. Jack let it ring fifteen more times before he decided to hang up and try again later.

"No answer," Jack told Rebecca

"Could the phones be down?"

"Can't be," Jack explained. "The PD's on their own grid. I'll try again in a little bit."

Rebecca got dressed in a pair of black jeans and a Boston Red Sox sweatshirt. She didn't have to worry about dressing like a cop; chances were she wasn't going to work today. Not with the snow as bad as it was. She put on a pair of fleece slippers and sat on the couch listening to the news, morning talk shows, even cartoons if they proved to be interesting enough.

Jack was still sitting at the table, doing nothing. Nothing at all. He hadn't missed a day of work in over a year. Never took a vacation or sick days. He was lost as to what to do if he couldn't get into work today. He could clean the basement, which he had been meaning to do for months now, but somehow never got around to it. He didn't think he could be like Rebecca and just forget about the real world and watch television all day. Watch a talk show about pregnant teenagers or about some over-paid actor making a new movie. He just sat there and wondered how the day should go.

It was almost eight o'clock before he decided to call the station again; but like before, a dozen rings and no one picked up. This was strange to say the least. It's the police station; someone should be there. Someone should pick up. He was going to use a last resort and dial 9-1-1 to see if he could get an operator.

*Ring.*

Someone picked up, "This call is being recorded. What's the emergency?" The operator said.

"Operator," Jack said, "I'm Detective Jack Stoughton of the Snow Hill P.D." He paused for a brief moment, "I've been trying to call the main number to the station and I haven't been able to get through."

"Officer, the lines are down from the storm last night. You're not the first one to call. Lines should be up soon."

"All right, operator," Jack said. "Thank you." He hung up the phone.

"Hey, Becca," Jack said from the kitchen.

"Yeah?"

"I just called emergency dispatch. Lines are down."

"Told ya so," Rebecca said jokingly.

Jack hadn't bothered to change into his usual work clothes. All he had on was a black shirt, red sweatpants, and socks. He wasn't going to bother getting dressed to go nowhere.

Jack got up from the chair and threw a crumb-filled paper towel in the trash. He walked over to Rebecca who was still sitting on the couch flipping through channels.

"Four hundred channels," Rebecca said "and not one good thing on."

"Isn't that how it goes?"

"Maybe I'll get on your computer," she suggested. "Find a cop chat room and meet some hot guys."

"You won't meet anyone as sexy as me," Jack told her, flexing his muscles.

They both laughed.

"What time did you get up this morning? I know you were up way before me."

"Around five. I couldn't sleep," Jack said. "I kept thinking about the cases."

"Yeah, me too," Rebecca admitted. "It's hard not to. I know you still don't believe me about what I saw."

"No, I do," he said. "I just find it hard to believe that you were shooting at some giant monkey."

"Damnit, Jack. It wasn't a monkey."

"Then what?"

"I don't know," she confessed. "It was ugly. Really, really ugly. I can't believe that damn thing didn't drop to the ground when I shot it four times."

Jack nodded, but didn't say a word.

Jack sat next to her on the sofa, put both hands on her shoulders, and began to massage her muscles, trying to relax the tension she'd been holding inside.

"Damn, that's good," she said.

"Faster, baby. Faster."

They both laughed again.

"Maybe you should try calling the station again," Rebecca suggested.

"It's only been twenty minutes since I tried," Jack said. "I'll wait an hour, at least."

Jack wanted to talk to her about moving in, but didn't know where to begin. He didn't want to tell her he was having financial struggles. That a cop salary wasn't enough to pay the bills and taxes for the house. He was lucky if he escaped with an extra hundred dollars a month. He even had to eat into his savings to refurbish the place and make it look decent, just as his father would have done, had he been alive today. But it was more than the financial situation. He loved her. He didn't say it much, but he did. He often thought about getting married to her, but wasn't quite sure if that's what she wanted. And the last thing he wanted to do was push her into such a strong commitment as that. They had been together for years now and he needed to work on one commitment at a time. First, moving in. If things went well enough, then marriage. That's the way he wanted it to be.

"So," Jack said, "have you given any thought to moving in yet?"

"Actually, I have."

"Is that good or bad?"

"It depends on how you look at it," she said, pausing for several seconds. "I think I could be moved in by March."

"Really?

"Yeah."

They kissed again … and again.

"I have to give the landlord a thirty-day's notice," Rebecca told him. "After that, I can start bringing my stuff in here."

"That'd be great," Jack smiled.

"Yeah it would," she smiled back at him.

Rebecca often thought back to her younger days; not that she was old now, but *younger*. Back in school; in her junior year, meeting Jack for the first time; then senior year when she fell in love with him. The college years were her favorite to think about. She thought of them as the best four years of her life, and maybe they were.

She first made love with Jack at a party that one of her roommates had for her twenty-first birthday. Rebecca and Jack got wasted that night, drinking tequila with beer chasers. They were drunk after the third throwback, but that didn't stop them from doing fourteen or fifteen or sixteen. She couldn't remember too well, but it was somewhere in the mid-teens.

Those years often took her back to her home … before her parents were murdered. She could still see her parents sitting at the kitchen table with different sections of the newspaper, drinking coffee. The grey vinyl tiles, the oak paneling with floral wallpaper; the kind that if you stared at it for too long you would become light-headed. The way the sun would filter in through the windows in the early mornings on beautiful spring days. She rarely thought about it much any more. It had happened a decade ago. She still felt guilty about it, not thinking about them as much as she thought she should. She could remember when the cops came to tell her. She was in the middle of a psychology exam when two officers came in and escorted her out to the hallway and told her the news. She'd never forget their names. The older officer was Sergeant Richard Griggs; his partner was Officer Martin O'Neal. She nearly collapsed. Jack was in her class, but he wasn't focused on the exam. He was watching Rebecca's movement from the glass in the door. He jumped out of his seat when he saw her stumble and one of the cops trying to hold her balance; he practically hopped onto desks until he made it out of the classroom to get to Rebecca, to find out what had happened. He was her strength through everything. No one had ever comforted her as Jack did. Not even Cliff Sullivan, who turned out to be a very wealthy lawyer. Jack was there for her, and she knew he would always be. That's why she chose him.

She sat there looking at Jack. She had never looked at another man like she did him. She never wanted to, never needed to. She knew how Jack felt even if he didn't express it as much as she would have liked. But in times when it mattered most, he made her feel loved like no one else had ever done.

"You want to try to go to work?"

"If we have to," Rebecca said. "*Only* if we have to."

"I'll call the station in a couple of minutes," Jack said. "If they say to stay home, then we will stay at home and sit on the couch all day watching soap operas."

She laughed, "It's a deal."

Jack went back to the kitchen to grab the phone.

*Ring.*

Jack picked up the phone on the first ring, "Hello?"

"Hey Jack," the voice on the other line said, "it's Roberts."

"Hey, what's going on, Greg?"

"Nothing," he said. "Just figured you were stuck at home as well."

"That I am."

"I bet you tried to call the station and couldn't get through, right?"

"Yeah," Jack said.

"Well, I got a guy who's plowing me out right now. He's in one of those front-end loaders. You want me to send him over your place?"

"That'd be good, actually," Jack told him. "Rebecca and I are stuck here."

"Rebecca, huh? Tsk-tsk."

"Yeah, yeah."

"I'll send him over," Roberts said. "Should be over there in about twenty minutes."

"Okay. Thanks Greg."

"You bet."

Jack hung up the phone. "Looks like we're going to be able to go to work, honey."

Rebecca walked into the kitchen, "Who called?"

"Greg Roberts," Jack said. "He's sending a plow over here to dig us out."

"Well, it's not too bad," she said. "At least we can get some work done."

Almost forty minutes went by before the plow guy came. He dug them out as best he could, making mounds of snow ten or even fifteen feet tall in the front yard. The driveway was smooth with only a tiny layer of snow stuck to the cement.
The snow had stopped and the sun was out, but the temperature was still the same; in the thirties.

It took almost a half-hour to make it back to the station. Jack went in the steel door on the side after Rebecca. They went right up to robbery/homicide. Only half the squad was there. Lieutenant Harrison was among the absent.

"What's going on boys?" Jack asked.

"Hey Jack," Martinez said

Martinez looked at the expression on Rebecca's face, "You wanted to stay home, huh?"

"More than you know," Rebecca told him.

"Boss ain't in yet?"

"No," Roberts said, exiting the coffee room. "Hasn't called in either."

Jack found his desk and sat down in front of a stack of papers. The large computer screen that occupied the most space had a yellow sticky-note stuck to the glass. CALL HUGH BROWN, the note read. Jack wanted to wait until at least ten or even eleven before attempting to call Hugh. Chances were he wasn't in yet and Jack didn't want to start working without having another cup of coffee.

Rebecca walked up and sat across from him at her desk.

Her desk was clean and clutter-free. She kept tall paper holders to separate forms and files. Everything else was organized in her desk drawers. The total opposite of Jack.

"Got a message," he told Rebecca, "to call Hugh."

"Anything important?"

"I don't know," he said. "It's probably about that green stuff we found at the crime scene. I'll give him a call in a minute. I want some coffee."

"Screw the cup of coffee," Rebecca said. "Let's go back to the country club. Something's not right with that place."

"Woman's intuition?"

"Maybe, but you should know by now, I'm always right."

"Yes dear," he nodded sarcastically.

# VII

January, 22nd, 2009 10:14A.M.

Kyle woke up, finding himself naked again with the sheets only covering a portion of his body, and not the portion he was hoping for if his parents came downstairs.

Kyle had been a nude sleeper for the last few years, always explaining to himself that it was because he felt more comfortable without the confines of pajama pants or a raggedy old shirt. On the other hand, Kennedy still had on a pair of Kyle's shorts and the baggy shirt.

She was still sleeping peacefully. Weekends were the time she made up for going to bed at midnight and waking up at six o'clock on school days. Now she could finally sleep in. Not that there was anyplace to go. And school was almost a certain closure for at least three or four days, or maybe the whole week. They hadn't been born yet during the blizzard of '78 when schools and businesses were closed down for weeks. Nothing was open and nothing was on the road. There was no doubt that a blizzard like this one would be in the history books for Massachusetts. It would probably be compared to the one that happened thirty-plus years ago to see which one came out stronger on the scales.

Kyle pulled the sheets over his crotch, looked up at the ceiling, and tried to go back to sleep, but he knew he wouldn't no matter how much he tried. The sun filtering in from the windows that surrounded the room was too bright. He had to get up to take Shadow outside to do his "business," as he called it. But before doing so, he would have to get the shovel out and make a path for him. He wasn't going to shovel the entire yard out, just a batch to his door that would maybe extend ten feet or so. Then he'd go help his dad with the driveway and the steps out front. Kyle was going to *try* to make it to the backyard shed and rev up the snow blower and grab a fifty-pound bag of rock salt to spread across the cement to break up the ice that had accumulated throughout the night.

Kyle waited another ten minutes, trying to recover from the long night, but his wait was futile.

He dressed in a basketball sweatshirt and dark sweat pants, and slid on his boots barefoot; he didn't bother to tie them.

He patted his leg. "C'mon Shadow," he whispered.

Shadow raced to him with a waving tail and a wide doggy smile.

Kyle bent down and kissed him on the top of his head, rubbed his belly, and led him to the door. He picked up a plastic shovel at the bottom of the stairs from a tall, slim cupboard.

"Shadow, wait a minute, then you can go out," Kyle said.

He opened the door and was astonished by the amount of snow buildup that surrounded. It was a slope of snow and his door was the highest part on this gradient.

He shut the door, walked back downstairs, put the shovel away, and whispered to Shadow, "maybe later."

Back in the bedroom, he took off his sweatshirt and placed it on top of the nightstand on his side of the bed; he left his sweat pants on when he got underneath the covers again.

Kennedy rolled over, facing him. "Good morning," she said.

"Good morning," Kyle had a child-like grin. "I think we're buried."

"The snow is that bad?"

"No," Kyle paused, "it's a lot worse."

Kennedy kissed him on the cheek, laid her head back

down on the soft pillow, and stared at the wall.

"You want some breakfast?"

"You cooking?"

"Of course," Kyle said.

"Then yes."

Kyle laughed and got out of bed, "It'll be ready in twenty, madam."

He went into the kitchen, figuring he would make some eggs and toast with a glass of orange juice. Something simple enough.

He grabbed a frying pan out from a cabinet, and a stick of butter out of the door console in the refrigerator, and began to prepare breakfast.

He turned on the television in the kitchen, a nice flat screen not bigger than thirteen inches. Kyle shuffled through the channels until he found a weather report estimating how many feet of snow had gathered overnight. "Two to three feet," the meteorologist said. "Some areas in central Massachusetts received as much as five."

"Holy shit," he whispered.

Too bad this snow storm happened here and didn't happen in Maine last year. He would have loved it. Maine was his favorite place to go. It was his retreat from stress and the rest of the world. Kyle had gone up there last winter with a couple of his friends. They went skiing, or at least his friends did. Kyle was too busy falling down after going ten feet down a hill. They tried snowmobiling, which was Kyle's *new* favorite thing to do. It was the best place to be in his opinion. He never wanted to leave the east coast for anything; however, he might travel to Colorado. He heard it was beautiful in the winter time, and real magical at Christmas, especially in the smaller towns. He was a winter fanatic, definitely zealous about it. The beginning of November to the end of March was his favorite time of year.

Most people felt the same way only because of Christmas, and he enjoyed Christmas just like the next person. Kyle would decorate his home with a tree lined with bright lights, a wreath on the door, and some decorative lights all around; he would take them down a few weeks later. He would get and give very well, sometimes giving expensive presents to his family and close friends.

That was something he loved to do. Like when he got his mother a pair of gold earrings, or bought his dad a new platinum watch. He loved to see the expressions on their faces when they unwrapped their gifts.

Kennedy crept up from behind, "Hey, sexy."

"Hey beautiful," he replied. "Breakfast is almost ready."

"Good, I'm starved."

"Well, according from the weather report," Kyle said, "we got about five feet."

"Five feet?" Her expression was mild.

"Yeah," he told her, placing four pieces of bread in the toaster. "After breakfast, I'm going upstairs to help my dad shovel, as I'm sure he will be asking me soon."

"Where's Shadow?"

"I think he's on the couch."

"Did you take him out?"

"No, I couldn't," he explained. "The snow is covering almost the entire door."

Shadow came from the living room upon hearing his name. He walked over to Kennedy and rubbed her bare leg.

"Hey boy," she patted his head and rubbed underneath his jaw, touching his tongue as it draped from his mouth.

Kyle removed the pan from the electric-range stove, "breakfast is served." He put the pan down on the countertop and took out a couple of dishes. He put some eggs on a plate for her with a couple slices of toasted bread and did the same for himself.

Kennedy took out a carton of orange juice from the top shelf in the refrigerator and placed it in the center of the table next to a pair of plastic cups.

Kyle brought the plates over with a fork on each dish, and sat down with Kennedy to eat their warm meals.

*Joseph McGee*

# VIII

Jack sat at his desk staring into space, thinking about the outcome of all of this. Going over every single detail in his head, trying to resolve these crimes. But he couldn't. Not in his head. He went back over the murder scenes again as if they were a blueprint running through his mind, or like a movie reel. He tried to identify with the victims, to ascertain exactly what it was they were doing and how they reacted to the intruder. Nothing made sense, though. There was no detectable forced entry in any of the scenes, which meant that they knew the killer. All the victims were members of that club, or at least those that had been identified so far. It didn't make sense. There was something at that club that was just iniquitous. Jack couldn't pinpoint it, but it was something. Something about the way they acted when they found out about Peter Long. He had to ask himself: *How would they react now with all of these other victims?* He didn't have the answer. When the streets were better, a little more interrogating would be in order.

Jack snapped out of his trance long enough to see Rebecca starring at him, but neither one said a word. It was as if they were both thinking the same thing. Maybe they had some sort of telepathic powers, or maybe it was just a gut instinct, or the fact that they had known each other and worked with each other for so long that made them so compatible as to just be indubitable with one another. That is what made good partners.

Jack finished his reports, signing all of them at the bottom to make it official, and threw them back in a drawer. He would give it to the secretary so she could store it in the computer and file it in one of those tall cabinets by her desk. He couldn't quite remember her name. She was new to the squad room, had only been there about four or five weeks. It was Jane or Janet or Janice. Something with a "J."

He knew he had to go to the country club, and it almost slipped his mind that he had to call Hugh Brown in the crime lab. Jack had to talk to Harrison too, but he wasn't in yet. Jack had many different things to do and all were very time consuming; he wasn't sure which order to do them in. He would rather talk to the Lieutenant first before proceeding with anything, but with his absence, Jack would have to skip that and call up Hugh, then head down to the club and bust some balls.

He reached for the phone, Rebecca watching his every move.

"Hugh," Jack said, "you wanted me to call you?"

"We ran that liquid we found."

"And?"

"It's blood," Hugh said.

"Blood?"

"It's different, though," Hugh explained. "It has over a hundred chromosomes."

"What does that mean?

"It's not human. I can't even tell what it is yet. The average human has forty-six chromosomes in their body. When you take one away or add it, it is usually a different species. But with this one, I can't quite be sure what this species is. It's unusual to say the least."

"Well, get back to me when you have something more," Jack told him. "Becca and I are going to follow a lead."

"I'll be in touch," Hugh said.

Jack hung up the phone.

"Well, it's definitely an alien," Jack said to Rebecca.

"Huh?" she said with a puzzled look.

"Hugh said something about too many chromosomes and it's not human."

"You're kidding, right?

"Nope."

"It could be a bug or a reptile for all we know," Rebecca considered. "Let's go check out that club. Think the streets are cleared?"

"They might be," Jack said. "It is on a main street after all."

"What if they're not?"

"I have an idea," Jack said, and got up from his chair. "I'll be right back."

Jack left the room and went downstairs to the first floor.

It was unusually quiet. Nothing but a hum from a far away printer and the silent whispers from the three men behind the counter.

Jack had never seen the lobby this empty before. It was the first time he noticed how dirty the vinyl tile was, and how ugly the taupe colored walls were. It was as if he were seeing it from someone else's eyes.

The sun grazed through the windows beautifully, blinding Jack as he walked to the counter, "Serge, is there a car on Bishops?"

"There should be," he said. "Just got a call of a fire on that street. Turned out to be a false alarm."

"Streets are cleared?"

"In that part of the city, yes."

Jack tilted his head, "Something's different about you."

"Everybody's saying that." Sergeant Andrews rubbed his new grey mustache.

"Ah, the mustache," Jack said. "Very professional look."

"Thanks Jack," he smiled. "If only my wife felt the same way."

Jack laughed.

Jack made some more small, non-work-related talk with the Sergeant before going back upstairs to join Rebecca and the rest of robbery/homicide.

"Talked to the sergeant," Jack said. "Should be cleared for driving."

"You ready?"

Jack stopped for a moment.

A million thoughts raced through his mind. He tried to separate his personal life from his professional one, but it was hard to do so when his personal life came with him to work every day. He knew he should concentrate on this case, to get it done fast, and not think about move-in arrangements with Rebecca. He needed to focus now. Get his head in the game before another body turned up dead.

"I was born ready," he said, shrugging his coat on. He picked out the keys from his pocket and tossed them to Rebecca. "You drive."

"How thoughtful of you," she said sarcastically.

"You know me," Jack said. "I'm always thoughtful."

* * *

Kyle stood out in the cold, the wind blowing the snow and covering his winter mask, then melting seconds later. The shovel jolted back a pile of snow and tumbled backwards. An uneven square was taking shape as Kyle put his strength behind each pull to lift up the heavy-packed snow.

Shadow was there beside him urinating on the almost-bare ground, but then he went in the house where it was nice and warm.

Kyle didn't bother to shut the door behind Shadow. He was going to give one more heave-ho to try and make the clearing a little bigger, then he'd go take a break for an hour to get out of those cold-wet boots and warm up.

The house was warm with the scent of spring, donated by the plug-in air fresheners placed strategically around the house. Something to take the smell of dog and dampness from the basement.

Shadow was chomping on a couple of doggie bones that Kennedy must have given him as Kyle came down the stairs. Shadow's body was laid out on the tile, unaware of anything but the tasty treat.

Kennedy walked out of the bathroom, hair dripping from the shower. She grabbed a white towel from around her neck and patted down her head. She wore Kyle's dark-blue plaid robe.

"Shower's all yours," Kennedy said to Kyle, watching him take off his face mask and gloves.

"Cool," he said, "but I'm not going to take one just yet. I want to take a break and then go shovel some more. I think I got a good path coming out. Maybe I can do a crop-circle in it."

"You going to help out your dad?"

"Yeah," he said. "In a little bit, I'll go. I'm too frozen to walk upstairs."

Kennedy went back to the bedroom to dress.

Kyle walked to the living room, kicked off his boots, and planted himself on the couch. After grabbing the remote from the coffee table he put his legs up and lay down, his head supported by the plush arm rest.

He sat for a while, then pressed down on the remote controls, the numbers reversing until they reached channel 7. The news. One reporter was out in the middle of the blizzard with police officers surrounding a house on a street that looked familiar to him, but he couldn't think of the name.

"The victims were brutally murdered," the woman said.

She carried on, explaining that the police were

investigating a murder and had no lead suspects.

*A murder? In Snow Hill?*

Murders didn't usually happen in Snow Hill. With heavy population a criminal element is expected. The population here was just over 30,000 people. He had never heard of a national news crew like NBC coming this way. The only time he could remember was a few years back in a neighboring city. Worchester's hospitals had nurses on strike and protesting with picket signs.

Almost thirty minutes had passed since he had kicked off his boots and lay down.

Kyle sat up, stretched, and wished he didn't have to go back outside.

He shut off the television and stood in the darkened room, fumbling for his boots so he could carry them into the kitchen.

Kyle turned to face Kennedy, but saw only an impressionistic version of her features through the dim light of the sun beating through the only two windows in the kitchen.

"What's wrong?"

"I just tried to call my parents," she said. "They're not picking up."

"Maybe they slept in late," he suggested.

She didn't say anything.

Seeing her like that brought back memories of a summer party they had both attended last year. It was the look on her face that made him think of it. It was the same look she got when she had too much to drink, a second before she vomited.

She moved next to him, looking out the window at the giant snowfield that stood before them. The house next door — Kennedy's old house — stood there, but it had never seemed so empty and peaceful and so scary at the same time. It looked dead. There was no liveliness to it. Vacant.

"Maybe I should go over."

"No, he said firmly. "The snow is too deep to walk across. Maybe they didn't answer the phone because they were shoveling."

Calmness seemed to come over her. "Yeah. That's probably it." She changed topics, "When you going to help your dad?"

Kyle was silent for a minute. "I'm not sure," he said finally. "I'm not sure."

They heard a plow in the street nearby. It might have been city workers, but Kyle thought it might have been his cousin, Barry.

Barry was a carpenter who built houses and decks and nearly everything for a home, but in the winter time when work was at its slow point he would use his Ford Explorer and do some plowing. Most people he knew liked him and his dad. He would no doubt get paid for it anyway. For a job like this, where there was so much snow, he would get maybe fifty bucks. Even though Barry might refuse it at first, he would accept it in the end.

Maybe Barry could plow the snow away from his door, Kyle thought. It would easily save him hours of struggling with mountains of snow with just him and a shovel.

Kyle walked to the bedroom to look out the window, trying to ascertain if it was his cousin or not, but the windows didn't show much more than snow; the view was egregious and dim.

He told Kennedy he was going upstairs to check on his parents, and if it was in fact his cousin outside with the plow. But when he got upstairs there was an unsettling silence that unnerved him and made him uneasy.

His parents were not around anywhere. Not in the kitchen having lunch or in the bedroom, perhaps doing something that Kyle did not want to see. He checked every room in the house. They were nowhere to be found.

*Maybe they were outside.*

He glanced out the window, but couldn't see his parents; but that was Barry plowing the snow away. He was doing a good job of it, too.

Kyle wasn't dressed to go outside and meet Barry; his boots were still downstairs in the kitchen and his jacket was hanging up by the door.

He made one final search of the house and determined his parents were not there. He couldn't get a good enough view from the windows to see if his mom and dad were outside shoveling, but the back steps looked cleared with just some grains of sand on them, and another small path that lead to the driveway that looked as if only a shovel could make such a trail. It had to be them. No tire tracks ran over the hard-packed snow. Plus, their car had been moved. They must have had to move the car so they could plow it. And that's probably where they were: in the street, still in their car, waiting to put it back. He figured that was the reason; there was no doubt about it. Although no one had asked him to move his truck, he would have. He would now.

Kyle ran down the stairs and threw on his jacket. Then he slipped on his boots and tied them tightly so that no excess snow or ice or water could penetrate his socks.

Kyle walked back upstairs and out the back door.

He jumped down the steps and walked through the tight path to his cousin. "Hey, Barry."

"Hey kid," he replied.

Kyle could tell not much had changed. Kyle hadn't seen him in a few months, but his features were still the same. A thin goatee faded at the top of his lip and his fiery-red hair was tucked underneath a navy-blue baseball cap with a bright-red B on the front to symbolize the Boston Red Sox.

"Where did your mom and dad go?"

"I thought they were outside with you."

"No, they mentioned that they had to pay someone and they'd be back in a little bit. They took their car and left. Wait. Didn't they have two cars?"

"Yeah, but one's in the shop. Something's wrong with the starter," he explained.

"Well, your dad had to buy a Lincoln, and those aren't cheap to fix."

"I know."

"Can you do me a favor and move your truck?"

"Sure. Can you also just push the snow away from my door, too? I tried to dig us out, but I didn't get too far."

"No problem," he smiled.

Kyle started up the engine with his automatic starter, opened the backseat to get the snow brush, and knocked the snow off his windows while Barry waited patiently for him to move.

As he shifted the car in reverse and parked it on the side of the street so Barry could complete the plowing he felt a slight twinge of unease about his parents being missing. Well, not missing, but gone. Where could they have gone in this weather? Not even a speck of dirt or cement could be seen on the street. Just a road of whiteness that glittered in the sunlight.

Kyle was going to sit in his truck until Barry was finished with the driveway and his door so he could return his truck to its parking place on the side of the house.

He pressed the window down and a cold gust of wind came rushing in so he put the window back up. "Too cold," he muttered to himself.

Almost a half-hour went by, and his parents did not return. Barry was nearly done now, just retracing his steps to

107

scrape the snow that he had missed previously.

Another ten minutes passed. Barry finished and Kyle parked the truck back in the driveway.

They made small talk for a few minutes, mostly making queries about Kyle's parents and where they could be. They said their good-byes and Kyle was back in the house by three-thirty.

He thought about calling his parents' cell phones, but decided against it. If they were not back by five o'clock then he would. But they should be back way before that, maybe any minute now. The snowy roads could be holding them back a bit as well. So Kyle waited.

# IX

January, 22nd, 2009 04:48P.M.

The wind was hard and relentless. A light haze of peach lit up the west side of the early-evening sky. It was a beautiful sunset despite the unbelievably cold temperatures that had dropped down into the single digits. It was a very cold day; a record-breaker. A light dusting of snowflakes fell for about an hour, but didn't accumulate more than an inch on the ground.

That night Kyle and Kennedy had snuck into bed a little earlier than usual. They were awakened by a loud knocking at the door. At first he thought it might be his parents for whatever reason.

But it wasn't.

Wearing only a short-sleeve shirt and pajama pants, Kyle opened the door.

He saw a tall man wearing a police uniform, "Kyle? Kyle Johnson?" The officer said.

"Yes."

"May we come in?"

*We?*

Kyle pushed to the side to allow their entrance.

He hadn't seen them before, but another man and a woman walked in behind the uniformed officer.

He didn't pay close attention to any of their features, just enough to know that the other two police officers were in plainclothes and looked as though they had been woken up as well, unexpectedly.

They walked down the stairs.

"You might want to have a seat, son." the plainclothed

109

man suggested. "I'm Detective Stoughton, that's my partner Detective Strong and this is Officer Welch." Detective Stoughton paused a moment.

Kyle wasn't sure if sitting down was something he wanted to do. In every television show he had ever seen, whether it be reruns of *NYPD Blue* or *CSI*, when the cop came to someone's house in the dead of night and asked someone to sit down it was *always* bad news. And seeing as how his parents hadn't come home and there was no answer on either of their cellular phones, Kyle feared for the worst.

Kyle pulled up a seat at the kitchen table and turned his head to see the time on the microwave. It read 2:18A.M.

Kennedy came in from the bedroom, "Kyle?"

He turned to face her and gave her an uncomfortable look; she returned the same features of uneasiness.

"Is this Kennedy Jensen?" Detective Stoughton asked

Before he could answer, Kennedy nodded.

She took a deep breath before she stepped forward and waited for the officers to tell her something egregious — like the things that were already floating in from the back of her mind, horrific things. She knew something bad had happened. She felt dizzy, as if she was going to faint and fall over to the kitchen floor, but she grabbed the back wall to maintain her balance.

Kyle started to jump out of the chair but hesitated. He kept a close eye on her as she walked over to sit beside him at the kitchen table.

Shadow crept in slowly from the living room.

"We stopped at your house first," Jack Stoughton said to Kennedy, "but no one answered. We found it more than a coincidence that the Jensen's house was in back of the Johnson's.

Stoughton and Strong used the other two chairs to sit down while Officer Welch stood, shifting his weight back and forth.

"Did something happen to my parents?" Kyle asked.

"Our parents," Kennedy amended.

"I'm afraid so," Officer Rebecca Strong said with a sympathetic smile.

Tears started to well up in her eyes. Kennedy looked at Officer Strong as if she was looking through her eyes to her soul. "What happened?"

"Both cars ran off the highway and crashed," Stoughton said. "No survivors." He looked uncomfortably around the room before turning back to Kyle. "I need to ask you some questions if that's okay. Just formal stuff," he promised.

"Where did you find them?" Kennedy asked, tears rolling down her cheeks.

"They crashed over the barriers of interstate two-ninety, near exit fourteen."

"They were in Worchester?"

"Apparently so," Officer Strong said. "Do you have any idea why they went out during the big snowstorm?"

"No," they both replied.

"Were your parents—"

Jack's phone rang. He excused himself from the questioning.

He thanked whoever it was for the call and returned, whispering something in his partner's ear.

Kyle thought it was suspicious, like maybe they were drinking or a drunk driver had forced them off the road. But it just didn't add up.

"Actually, I'm sorry we wasted your time."

"What are your talking about? What's going on?" Kyle demanded.

"It looks like we have to investigate this as a homicide," Officer Strong said.

Kennedy and Kyle's features of sadness and anger soon

faded to impassive.

Rebecca and Jack stood up from their seats.

"You're eighteen, right?" Stoughton asked Kyle.

"Yes."

"May we check upstairs — your parents' house?"

"For what?" Kyle looked at Detective Strong, dumbfounded.

"Your parents seem to be linked to ..."

"Jack!" Rebecca yelled.

"Jesus. It's the kids' parents, Rebecca," Jack said, then turned to face Kyle. "They seem to be linked to a series of murders that have been happening recently. I have one last question for you, but I think I already know the answer to it." Jack paused and pushed in the kitchen chair. "Did either of your parents belong to the Snow Hill Country Club?"

They both nodded.

"Ms. Jensen, may we search your home as well?"

"Of course," she said. The tension seemed to shut off, but for only a moment.

As Rebecca took out her cell phone and walked to the doorway to have a more private conversation, Jack put his hand on Kyle's shoulder. "I promise I'm going to nail the son-of-a-bitch responsible for this."

Kyle felt assured of that somehow. He knew that the officer would do his best to get the bastard responsible for his parents' deaths. Kyle's head filled with anger and fear; sorrow would undoubtedly come later. He fought back the tears, turned to the refrigerator, and took out a small bottle of water. He gulped a large portion down and stood it back on the refrigerator's door.

He wanted to fall to his knees and cry, to sob for the loss of his parents, and pray ... pray that this was something surreal. That this was just some horrible nightmare he had suffered. A nightmare that at any moment he would awake from with cold sweat on his forehead like he used to get after watching horror movies when he was younger. But something inside him knew it wasn't a dream. This was real life and it was really happening to him and to Kennedy. Kennedy. He had almost forgotten that she had suffered the same loss. He walked over to her and hugged her, kissing her cheek twice, and whispering, "I love you." She nodded and began to cry harder.

"I can't believe this," she sobbed.

"It's okay, baby. I'm here," he assured her. "We're going to get through this together."

Officer Strong returned moments later, "Another team is coming to search the other house," Rebecca told Jack.

"Good. You take Ms. Jensen and head over there. Welch and I will check upstairs.

"Ms. Jensen?"

"Kennedy," she corrected through tear-filled eyes.

"Kennedy, could you please show me around your house? We want to do a thorough investigation."

Kennedy didn't want to leave, but Kyle convinced her to assist them. He knew they wanted to catch the person behind this. He only hoped that when they found him they didn't handcuff him and bring him to prison where he would receive the full amenities of a gym and a meal three times a day on taxpayers' money. He wanted them to place a bullet into his head, in the center of his eyes, and let him fall to the ground like the sack of shit he was. Kyle would even offer to be the shooter. He wouldn't offer. He would *insist*.

\* \* \*

After Rebecca and Kennedy left, Jack and Kyle remained seated at the table, and Welch sat now, too.

Jack explained the seriousness of the case and exactly what had happened. He wasn't supposed to tell a victim's child but he felt close to Kyle for some odd reason. Close as if he were a younger brother ... or a son.

*A son?*

Jack shuddered the thought away.

Jack and Kyle walked upstairs and went straight to the bedroom. Officer Welch went into the kitchen to search for anything that might be of use, even though Jack knew he wouldn't find anything.

They had already found the handprints on the trunk of both totaled cars. Jack wasn't sure exactly what he'd hope to find. Probably nothing. A bunch of personal effects that only mean something to the victims.

He looked at Kyle who was on the verge of tears. Jack could see his chin was quivering, as if he was too scared to cry. But crying might be the one thing he needed to do right then, not helping him and Rebecca solve this case by ushering the cops around his dead parents' home looking for nothing ... or something.

Jack took notice of water marks that resembled shoe prints, boot prints. Probably a size ten. A trail led from one of the windows in the living room to the bedroom.

Finally, Kyle took notice as well.

"What are ..."

Jack shushed him, took his gun out of its holster, and wrapped both hands around the handle. He walked slowly to the bedroom, silently praying that the floor didn't squeak.

Jack held Kyle back with his right arm as he snuck up on the door, then he gently touched it open with the toe of his boot.

No one was inside, but someone had been there. The entire room was in shambles. Clothes were mounted on the floor; the mattress was overturned against the wall. Papers and magazines were spread across the plush carpet, and furniture was torn and smashed to pieces. The rest of the house looked as though it had never been touched; perfect and clean. In contrast, the bedroom looked as if a small tornado had erupted, causing massive damage to anything around. Even the television tube was smashed. It was complete chaos.

"Holy shit," Jack whispered.

Jack looked around the room, but knew that assailant had already left.

"Find anything?" Jack asked.

"No," he said from somewhere in the house.

Jack turned his head to face Kyle. "You didn't hear anything?"

"No. I was asleep," he told Jack.

"When did you fall asleep?"

"About four hours ago. I think it was just after ten o'clock."

Jack turned away, reached for his cell phone, and called Rebecca.

"Hey, Becca. The bedroom is torn to shit. Somebody was looking for something."

She told him they found the same thing on her end; he could hear Kennedy crying in the background.

"Something else interesting," she told him. "I just got a call from the station. Each victim had at least one child that was reported missing."

"Missing?"

"Yeah. Every victim had children missing."

"What about Mrs. Long?"

"Yeah, same thing. Her eldest son was nine years old … and missing."

"I think we should take the kids with us to the station or somewhere," Jack told her. "I just have a really bad feeling about this."

"You know the rules, Jack. It's up to them if they want protection."

"I know," he said. "I'm going to look around some more then we're going to get out of here."

Jack hung up the phone.

"Kyle," Jack said, walking back into the room.

"Are you an only child?"

Kyle looked at him, confused. "Yes," he whispered.

"And your girlfriend?"

This time he nodded.

"Kyle, I need you to come with me," Jack said.

He didn't know how to tell Kyle, or even what to tell him. Was he supposed to tell him what Rebecca had told him? Jack didn't know if either Kyle or Kennedy could handle something like that right now. He didn't want to just drop them off at the station and tell them to wait by his desk while he went to investigate their parents' deaths some more. He didn't want to bring them to that kind of environment but he couldn't leave them there either. Whoever had come here could easily come back again. But what if they didn't want to come? What would the option be? To put out a couple of patrol cars? It was pitch-black outside with mounds of snow all the way around. Jack didn't want to take the chance of anyone else dying or getting hurt. Not if he could prevent it.

Jack helped Kyle off the bed. "Listen, Kyle," Jack said. "I know this is hard for you, believe me I do, but I think who ever came here might came back for you. I just have a bad feeling. You can't stay here."

Kyle looked up at him, tears finally streaming down his cheeks. He nodded and left the room.

Jack followed him.

"Welch, c'mon," Jack said.

Officer Welch checked that all the doors were locked before going downstairs to join Jack and Kyle.

Kyle sat on his bed with Shadow lying next to him as he put together three day's worth of clothes and tied them in a plastic grocery bag. A few minutes later Rebecca and Kennedy came in.

"You're taking us to the police station?"

"No," Jack said, "somewhere else."

Jack smiled and nodded as Kennedy walked past him to sit with Kyle on the bed.

Jack went over to Rebecca and told her what he had planned. He wasn't going to take them to the police station. It wasn't right for a victim to be forced out of his home like this. Jack was going to invite both of them over to his house, to stay in the guest bedroom. He knew it wasn't much, but it was better than the station. It was something he had never done before, but there was nowhere else to go. The city might pay for a hotel room and have a patrolman sitting outside the door but the storm was just too bad to travel to any of the three hotels in Snow Hill. Besides, it would only be for a day or two, maybe three, tops.

Rebecca agreed to go along with the plan. She wasn't overjoyed about it and she didn't know what the Lieutenant would say to it. He might go along due to the storm outside, and he might not. But, technically, if Kyle and Kennedy both agreed to do it, then it was out of law enforcements' hands.

Kyle must have told Kennedy, because she was packing a bag of clothes of her own. She got her hair care products out of the bathroom, and packed some toothpaste and a toothbrush and a comb.

Jack walked into the bedroom. "You guys ready?" he asked with a congenial look.

Neither replied.

This was obviously too arduous for either of them to handle. In a way, Jack was uneasy about the whole situation, and for the first time in a long time he felt tongue-tied and unable to comfort Kyle or Kennedy.

Jack had never had to deal with something like this before. If a murder occurred, he would tell the victim's closet relative (which was usually the victim's spouse) and that would be the end of it. If the victim had children, he would hand out a business card for a child psychologist, and he would do nothing more to comfort them. He often felt guilty. He hoped that over time it would get easier to tell people that someone they loved had died, but he knew it never would. This time might be his chance to actually help the victim's family by not letting them become victims themselves.

They arrived at Jack's house almost an hour later. Jack slid the patrol car into the garage and Kyle parked his truck off to the side in the driveway; if Jack had to get out there would be plenty of room to squeeze by.

Kyle insisted that he bring his truck with him. Jack wasn't quite sure why. In fact, he didn't think Kyle was stable enough to drive the thirty minutes it took. But it was a slow drive and he made it there safely, Kennedy too.

The wind was brittle at three-forty in the morning. Not a single car was out on the road that any of them could see. A light dusting of snow began to glitter down to the street. The news claimed it shouldn't accumulate to another inch.

Jack had just hung up the phone with the station. Harrison was out, but he talked to one of the night detectives on duty and told him the situation. He assured Jack that he would let the Lieutenant know. Jack hung up the phone and checked on the kids in the spare bedroom next to Jack's. They were sleeping, and by the looks of it they had fallen asleep crying.

Rebecca was still awake, lying in bed in her night-clothes

underneath the covers, waiting for Jack to get in beside her and shut off the lamp.

Jack kicked off his shoes, loosened his belt, slid his pants to the floor, and took off his shirt. Before getting into bed Jack opened the blinds and looked outside. The snow had faded until it finally vanished in the night's sky.

Jack pulled the covers over himself, kissed Rebecca on the cheek, and said goodnight to her as he turned off the lights.

*Joseph McGee*

# X

The crescent moon faded over a clear sky. The wind was cold and heartless, and blew debris of snow from side-to-side, first in small coatings, then hustling into a fury and creating miniature tornados. In the few minutes before dawn, the snowfall had finally ended. Kyle and Kennedy still slept in the guest bedroom under the three layers of blankets that Rebecca had made ready for them to use the night before.

Jack was the first to wake up to the light hum of his alarm clock that sat on the nightstand, glowing a colorful green. He threw on his blue robe, stepped into his fleece slippers that he had bought at L.L. Bean, and made his way downstairs, silently.

The sun was creeping over the hills just about now, glaring its powerful rays through the windows. The temperature was increasing slightly into the upper thirties. It might reach the high forties by midday, but it wouldn't get any warmer than that.

Jack sat down at the kitchen table. He didn't bother to see if the morning paper had arrived yet or not. If it did, it would be somewhere in the few feet of snow; the carrier never seemed to get it on the porch no matter how many times Jack called to complain.

He stared blankly, waiting for the coffee to brew in the machine on the counter.

Jack felt like going back to sleep, as he did every morning at this time. It was 7:15, according to the microwave's digital clock. He folded his arms down on the table and planted his head in between, wishing the coffee to hurry up.

He expected to see Rebecca coming down the stairs next, which reminded him of that commercial: *The best part of waking up is Folgers in your cup.*

It was Kyle instead who came down in a white tank top and red flannel boxers. Either he had forgotten that this wasn't his home or he just didn't care enough to get dressed this early in the morning. He was nearly a spitting image of Jack, and had he not had two guests in his house, he'd be wearing something very similar.

"Good morning," Jack said to Kyle.

"Morning," he grunted

"There's some coffee in the pot if you drink it. If not, there should be some hot chocolate in the cabinet," Jack pointed.

Kyle went to use the bathroom down the hall on the left. When he returned he fumbled through the cabinet for some hot chocolate mix.

Kyle set a mug of tap water in the microwave on high for a minute to get it steaming. Then he joined Jack at the table. He poured the mix into the cup, stirring it well, and took a careful sip. A soft chortle came from his lips; a look of disdain smudged his face as if he had burnt his tongue.

Jack was not sure if he should strike up a conversation or let it go as he stood to get his coffee fix.

Jack waited until seven-fifty to call the station and update the Lieutenant on what happened but Harrison still wasn't in. Detective Robbins picked up the phone and assured him that he would tell the Lieutenant word-for-word.

"When Rebecca wakes up," Jack paused, "we're going to go out for a while. You gonna be okay by yourselves?"

"Investigating my parents' murders?" asked Kyle

"Yes."

"I want to come."

"I can't allow that," Jack told him.

"I deserve to go, too," he lashed out. "I need to go, Jack. Please."

"You can't. If anything were to happen.... If something happened to you.... You can't."

He could tell Kyle understood his unspoken reasoning, but he still wasn't happy with the decision. Surprisingly, he wanted Kyle to tag along too. But logical thinking won the argument in his head. He couldn't allow the kid to go. He wasn't a cop. He did not have special training. He was a high school senior, nothing more.

At eight-thirty, Rebecca was still comfortably asleep. Jack decided to let her sleep a little longer. If she was still conked out by ten, then he would wake her and they could leave the house by eleven or eleven-thirty.

Eleven-thirty came and Rebecca was barely awake, snacking on a cold piece of toast, sitting at the kitchen table in her purple fleece bathrobe.

Jack had just hung up the phone with Kennedy's closest relative—an aunt from Chicago. He had explained what had happened and the aunt agreed to be there by Wednesday. She was driving up from North Carolina and would take a couple of days to arrive. He assured her that he personally would watch over her niece for the time being.

Kennedy would be turning eighteen soon, but by law, Jack had to notify the closest living relative or Child Protective Services.

Jack sat across from Rebecca, watching her slowly sip the hot coffee, and wondered if Kyle had gone back to sleep or stayed up wondering what was going to happen when he and Rebecca left for work.

Noon had just passed and Rebecca was slipping into some dungarees and fastening her holster to the belt. "Almost ready," she yelled down the stairs before she remembered that the kids might still be sleeping. She was finishing lacing her high-grade boots when a loud explosion erupted from outside with enough force to rattle the windows, sounding like a thunder cloud.

She shrugged on her parka in a hurry and rushed downstairs expecting to see a car accident or a house blistering in flames. "Jack?" She called out, but received no answer. "Jack?" she tried again.

He came running in from the garage, "Rebecca!"

They met in the kitchen with not a light on. The power had gone out subsequent to the loud noise, but not a single window rattled again, nor did the kitchen shriek with tipped-over cups or dishes. It was unnervingly quiet. Jack clearly knew that something was wrong.

Rebecca said, "What the hell was that?"

"I don't know," Jack answered.

A scream ricocheted downstairs like a shotgun blast, piercing through the dead silence. It was a woman's cry. It was Kennedy. Through the ceiling tiles, they could hear an aggressive struggle.

Jack and Rebecca ran up the stairs together, pulling their weapons out; Jack jiggled the doorknob but it was locked. A sudden rush of terror overwhelmed him. He stood back, putting his fear to the side, raised his gun, and fired two rounds at the lock, shattering it into chips of metal and splinters of wood. Rebecca pushed her weight through the door first; Jack blasted in right behind her, ready to shoot some assailant.

The room was empty of people, save Kyle and Kennedy. There were no trespassers in the room; no broken windows or any signs of intrusion. It was the first thing Jack looked for as he swept around the room, pistol aimed eye level.

Kennedy was in tears; Kyle was bleeding from the mouth.

"It's gone," Kyle groaned, holding his mouth to catch the

blood.

"Who was it? Where'd they go?" Jack asked impatiently.

"I don't know," Kyle said. "I don't even know what the fuck it was."

"It?" Rebecca chimed in.

"It was tall, black as night. It had a tail and it made this awful noise," Kyle started recalling it; in is mind, he could still see it appearing as if from nowhere and slithering around like a snake, sticking to shadows of the room.

Jack holstered his weapon. "Becca, can I see you for a minute?" He pulled her off to the side. "Did you mention anything to them about what you thought you saw?" he whispered.

"I didn't mention a damn thing to them," she promised. "I'm telling you I saw something, and it was not fucking human, and they saw it too. There's your proof. I'm not insane"

"Then what was it?" he asked disdainfully.

"I don't know," she answered earnestly, "but I may know someone who might."

"Who?"

"I'll explain later," she told him and returned her attention back to the kids.

They were on the ground. Kyle held Kennedy's head in his arms as she released more tears. It was all she could do. The only comfort she felt was in the arms of the one she loved. He had risked his life to save her from whatever it was that came into that room, whether man or beast; he showed courage and nearly sacrificed his life for her. That was something he always swore he'd do for her, but she never thought he'd have the courage to actually go through with it if the situation ever warranted it.

Jack went to the windows on the other side of the room, his big stern face frowning as he looked through the snow for any footprints. Of course there were none. It was clean and untouched like the deepest desert sand.

*Rebecca and the kids couldn't have imagined the same thing, could they?* Jack was puzzled now, confused in an epic portrayal of a cop with too many inconclusive pieces to fit in this maddening puzzle of murder and mystery. He stood there, arms by his sides, waiting like a fat kid trying out for the high school basketball team, knowing he would not be picked. Jack would not figure this out. There was something behind the grey lines, something he couldn't put color to. People were dying. People with no obvious connection except belonging to the same club that countless others had joined in the past years. If Jack figured correctly with his cop instinct, there would be others who would be murdered. Whoever or *whatever* was committing these murders would not soon stop. That was plain to see. And Jack would risk his last breath to bring the bastard to jail for twenty-five to life.

* * *

Kyle worried about Kennedy, about Jack and Rebecca, and about himself. Shadow was kept in the bedroom, and he would surely protect his owner from any ominous intruder wishing to do harm. He was loyal that way, more loyal than any of Kyle's friends.

They were staying in. This house was now a bunker, a safe haven surrounded by mounds of snow.

Silence engulfed the house. For hours, no one spoke; no one dared to. It was a testament to exactly what was happening. Kyle thought they might find peace in solitude, but tranquility was not to be had.

Something desperately needed to be done, and without reasoning or rational thinking, Kyle knew what it was.

He would do some snooping. There was no telling what Jack would do to Kyle if he caught him flipping through folders and papers and launching his own investigation on his parents' deaths. It wasn't the most common thing for a high school senior to do, but under the circumstances, any kid in any place in the world who had lost their parents under such traumatic conditions, would want it too—killing the bastard who murdered the ones they loved. Kyle flashed images about some of the most devastating acts in his lifetime: 9/11, when those terrorists had killed thousands of innocents; the Virginia Tech incident when a gunman went on rage and killed over thirty people. He felt as much rage and anger as both those days—and twice as frightened. He was now alone, but he had Kennedy by his side. They would live as good a life as anyone could. She was parentless just as Kyle was; she would lean on him as much as she could and would give anything if he did the same. His sturdy determination to not need anyone was coming on full blast—she couldn't understand that about him sometimes. But she would be there for him to cry on when he needed her, although she couldn't remember ever seeing him cry.

She didn't want him to go off and hide, but she feared what he'd reveal if he let anyone in right now.

* * *

The night was a moonless one. The snow had stopped, but the wind promised that it was going to stay cold and wet for a while. The house was silent save for the crackling of the wood in the fireplace. Jack tried to relax in his recliner, sipping on a warm mug of coffee, and reading a book by Greg Olsen. His mind ran for a moment, his eyes still following the words on the page but not penetrating his deep thoughts. He was in his night-pants and white T-shirt. The fireplace was keeping him warm and he contemplated sleeping in the recliner. The heat was cranked up in the entire house; he had put the thermostat up to eighty. Around midnight or so, he'd drop it by ten degrees, and that would suffice for the rest of the night until morning. Jack hated to even think about his next gas bill.

Jack couldn't sleep and his eyes were too tired to carry on with another page in his book. He walked around the house, checking every door and every window, making sure all were latched and locked securely. The city was crippled right now, that was not to say that the force hasn't borrowed some snowmobiles to get through in case there was an emergency. There hardly was any kind of a criminal emergency; medical emergencies were another story. There's no predicting when someone's going to have a heart attack after all.

Still stuck in his mind were the employees at the country club. Like an angry parent, he loomed over every inch of the place in his thoughts, mapping a plan of attack.

# XI

January 24th, 2009 05:30A.M.

With gleam in his eye, Kyle sat in the chair opposite the bed, watching Kennedy sleep. He'd been awake for the past three hours wondering what would have happened if he couldn't get that thing off of her. It reminded him of that classic movie from the '70s, *Alien*; the way it looked and moved, its coated skin, and the horror it seemed to carry around with it like an aura of spirits. Though the nightmare was over, for now anyway, he thought *what if it happens again? What if I'm not there to help her? What if she dies in front of my eyes and I can't do a damn thing about it?* Those were the most terrifying questions he had ever asked himself—and before too long, he had made a plan. It wasn't original. It wasn't the most brilliant of schemes. He was going to find out what this thing was and kill it before it killed anyone else, even if it meant losing his own life in the process.

It was a big sacrifice for such a young man to give, and he might never fully understand how that would ultimately affect everyone else around him, even Jack and Rebecca who might never get to know Kyle completely, leaving the slight possibility lingering in the back of their minds about what would have become of him had he grown into a man, or perhaps creating remorse and guilty feelings that they could have done something to prevent his death.

Tears welled in his eyes as he thought of his parents; the last time he saw them upstairs when he had asked his father for the ring to give to Kennedy. He remembered seeing the twinkle in his father's eyes when he handed it over, knowing that he had made a wise choice. He never said much, but Kyle could tell in his voice that he was swollen with pride over the man he had raised. Nothing could ever shake that moment.

His breath caught. Kyle struggled to breathe through the whiny shutters of uncontrollable sobs. Then he began to hyperventilate because he was still trying to be quiet for the sake of Kennedy's sleep. He clutched his chest, willing himself to pull himself together, to be calm. He forced himself to the floor. After a short while, he got enough control of his breathing to where he didn't feel like he was going to lose consciousness; the wooziness had run its course.

Kyle crawled away and slipped into the shadows of the corner. He raised his knees to his chest and cried softly. It was the first time that he had really been scared for his future, for his life and the people around him, like it was all *his* fault. It wasn't, of course. He had nothing to do with any of this, but to him that didn't matter much. He just knew his parents were dead and Kennedy's parents had been killed after he had cleaned her father's clock with a clean punch. And now she had been attacked.

His tears flowed until dawn.

The sun rose brightly into the sky, as if God Himself was speaking to Kyle and telling him better days were to come. But he wasn't so sure if he could see the silver lining through all that had happened.

As the sun sneaked in from the windows; Kennedy softly stirred to her other side, avoiding the sunlight. Kyle treasured his memories as they came unannounced, like a clear sky breaking through a stormy day. He realized that when everything was all said and done, when he finally returned home with Kennedy, everything would be different. It would all be a reminder to him, whether it was dusting bookshelves, cooking dinner, or playing with Shadow. He was about to embark upon the worst days of his life—and he knew it. As the hours passed by, as the days faded into one another, Kyle would forever be inundated with memories of what he had lost.

He knew Jack had gotten a hold of the police station last night and they'd send people around once the roads were cleared some, but it seemed like it would never happen. Kyle wanted one of Jack's guns to slip behind his waistband in case whatever it was came back, whether it be mutant or a man in costume. That *sonofabitch* would not be so lucky next time.

Kyle hadn't known Jack for long, but he figured he'd be downstairs sipping on some coffee and eating lukewarm toast while waiting for Rebecca to either wake up or shower. It being so early, Kyle guessed Rebecca was still asleep.

The thought was always on the surface of Kyle's mind: *What if Kennedy was killed and blood had stained the walls like in one of those survival-horror video games?* Kyle could've been hanging by his balls from the ceiling, literally.

Kyle yawned, scratched his head, and sat on the chair as he had last night, waiting for Kennedy to wake up. He felt as though he had slept and dreamed during his time of crying and worrying. And for some reason, his head kept replaying his parents' voices, but old and decomposing like long forgotten memories. He hoped to God that he would never forget their sound or the way they looked. Then he remembered he'd have to see them once more. Kyle had yet to identify the bodies. Though they had picture identifications with them, it was customary for recording purposes that a spouse or close family member would point at them through a television monitor and say yup or nope. It wasn't like some television shows where they roll the body out on a metal tray and reveal their face from a thin blue white sheet, looking pale and peaceful.

Kennedy blinked her eyes open. With one hand she reached behind her, frantically searching for Kyle. She whipped her body around and saw him sitting there, head in his hands, and asked, "Kyle, what's wrong?"

He looked at her, smiled, and said, "Nothing's wrong. Go back to sleep." He hoped his voice was reassuring and didn't give itself away.

Kyle stood up, knowing that something was very wrong, that *he* was about to do something very wrong. "I'll be right back," he promised Kennedy.

He made a mental checklist: gun, police reports, find his parents' murderer.

\* \* \*

After the man was dead, and his burning flesh extinguished, the large concrete room filled with the stench of cooked skin. He was sprawled out on a wooden X, his wrists and ankles bound with thick, knotted rope. The smoke from his darkened corpse drifted lazily in the air, attracting flies and other small insects that could digest Mr. Borneman. After all, Borneman had it coming, George Miller thought to himself. If you can't pay your dues, then don't join, that's what he always said. He ran the show. Around here, he was king, a god even, the ruler of these four walls, and the one guy you did not want to fuck with while walking down a dark alley. His thin build and regal upbringing had no consequence in the deepest, darkest part of his soul, a place that might have born resemblance to Satan himself. He had made a deal with the devil and the devil repaid him in full by giving him this opportunity to set things right again in this town.

Very few people knew the secret, and even fewer decided to question it. Was it Satan and his dominions? Not sure. Was it some god that was cursed on this sacred land? Possibly. Only one man knew the truth.

George Miller.

He went from being a gentle soul to a man without a conscious; his trials reaped no consequence no matter how severe or benign his actions might be. To him, he was invincible, able to withstand a .45 slug to the head, or even the end of the world. And he knew it. As long as he did what he was told, and was a "good little soldier," as his dad had called him when he was much younger, he would survive it all.

Borneman's skin, like a roasted pig, flailed upward; cooked insides and boiled blood dripped down. He was just one of the many whose dues were not up to date.

Miller walked out of the cold concrete room. The smell of death lingered heavily in the hall, as it always did. One could not help but smell the awful odor, whether it be urine from a 'behind-dues' member pissing in fear or shitting himself while he was being tortured or burned alive until his final screams were drowned out by the crackle of flames and melting flesh.

Miller had pleased Him again. He was one with Him, connected somehow, like a vampire to its sired souls.

There were more people to collect from before the final phase could take place and He would then be released from His prison, what Miller knew as the Outerworld.

Before taking on his management role, George Miller had been told three things. One was about the different worlds, or rather the same world; two, about what would happen if he did as he was told; and three, his riches and failings.

As smug as he was, Miller thought there was only one world. But he was wrong. There was not just one world: there were many, many different Earths, as it had been explained. Like a snowflake, no two were ever the same. Yes, they might share similar qualities, but one little change in life, one little derailed track would alter the future significantly.

And Miller looked forward to the riches he was promised when his deed was done.

# XII

January 25th, 2009 07:22A.M.

The sky cut open, revealing a side of pure light, like wildfire spreading through the white clouds of the heavens, while the other side remained ash-grey — the devil's playground.

Kyle had been a kid who never expected trouble, but somehow would reluctantly find it wherever he went. When he was seven years old, he climbed the tall oak tree in Snow Hill Park and fell, luckily only spraining an ankle. At twelve, he was caught with his father's cigarettes, though, fortuitously, shortly thereafter his father had quit the bad habit once and for all. Kyle knew things had a reason in life, no matter which path he took. But this time, trouble had found him again.

Kyle looked out the window. Kennedy still slept under a crisp cotton blanket and a warm fleece throw. He looked out at the sun, staring into the great beyond — or in God's eye, and thought to himself for the umpteenth time *what the hell is going on?*

He was tired of questioning himself, tired of playing scenarios out in his head like life was a damned video game. Kyle was finally starting to accept his parents' deaths — and the death of Kennedy's parents. And sooner or later they'd both have to go down to the medical examiner's office and identify the cold carcasses of their families.

Abruptly, the dark clouds hovered over everything, covering the light in utter dusk.

A storm was on the rise. A bad one. Maybe as bad as the one just two days ago. *It can't be worse than the last one, can it?*

The gloomy shadows created by the sky's tempting malevolent characteristics made it seem like it was the end of the world; and a large, crashing ball of fire would make its way downward creating the end of time for all of humanity, as it once did a long time ago for dinosaurs.

The dim light seemed to be pressing itself up against the window, as if it were a living, breathing being, trying to break in and grab hold of both him and Kennedy.

That's what he was afraid of the most.

Losing her. The one he loved. The only person left to care about him. He couldn't let anything happen to her, not on his life.

Kyle was tired, but he couldn't sleep. He never left the bedroom; never let on that he was awake, that things were troubling him. To be honest, he was surprised that Kennedy could sleep, though her parents probably had it coming in more than one way. They were mean, nasty *sonsofbitches*. He thought of exhausting himself, methodically wearing himself out, until he couldn't drag his ass to take a crap. Maybe then he could sleep.

It was a quarter-past eight when Kyle finally decided to get up and dressed. Through the thin walls, he heard Jack and Rebecca in the other room, talking, but it was too faint to make any words out. He put on a wool hat and heavy coat and exited the bedroom quietly, not disturbing Kennedy's sleep. He stuck to the shadows, sliding down the hall as if he were invisible. Had there not been sconces to light the pathway, he might've been just that.

Kyle knew of only one place to get answers, and he'd have to beat the storm if he wanted to get there without freezing to death on the streets. Climbing over snow banks, dodging minimal traffic, and watching his footing over icy patches came almost as a second nature to him. He was used to all the oblique weather conditions Snow Hill had to offer; the last few years of winter had produced ghastly snowstorms, raging from November until the end of April; and still, in the beginning of May, there'd be slush piles and melting trickles of snow and ice in the streets running into the sewage system.

With no transportation other than his own two legs, nature would be his greatest combatant for the moment.

Leaving the house from the front, the mound of snow was well over the stairs. Throwing caution to the wind, he leapt over the half-foot of snow that engaged the top step. He landed on his stomach, hard enough to draw the wind from his lungs.

As he glanced around, every street looked the same; every yard had the same identical white powder. He made his way out the front walkway, clearing the chain-link fence by a good, clean foot. He was standing above the city, towering over everything that stood less than four feet high. Grey puffs formed in front of his mouth as he tried to steady his breathing. He carried himself to the end of the street, looked right, then left as if he expected cars to race speedily down the intersection. Of course, that was impossible, and still would be for weeks; they'd be lucky if the entire town wasn't buried alive under a mountain of snow, leaving rotting corpses to thaw out in late spring. Kyle had always thought that the stranger things were, the more likely they were to happen.

***

Before Jack could realize the notion of monsters or even ghosts, he knew that something about this was special, peculiar. Strange in a way that he knew no other cop on this planet had had to face. What was unique about it? There were several dead bodies. Some mutilated in a blood soup, some made to look like a suicide. They were all killed in various ways, some more

137

grotesque than others. Someone at that club wasn't being completely honest. Jack's hardworking years on the force told him that. He'd interviewed rapists to murders to run-of-the-mill muggers, and each came with a different sob story of why they did what they did and would never do again, swearing on their mother's life just to end up back a few months later with the same old *Oprah* story. He often joked about that they should turn the station house into a television center for reality TV. They'd make a fortune on these crackerjacks doing the wrong thing, swearing they'd never do it again, then a little while later ending up behind bars with strike number three.

That's the way it sometimes went, Jack supposed.

He stretched and got out of bed, planting his feet into his slippers by his bedside. He walked to the window and looked out at the pure while blanket of snow that seemed to cover the entire Earth in one big swallow. It was like looking at a brilliantly white wall for a long period of time and hurting your eyes from the constant stare.

Thinking he was letting the kids and Rebecca sleep late, he went into his den, sat in his favorite recliner, and tried to relax his head against the cushion. The fire had gone out but the heat from the radiator kicked on at seventy-four. He wrapped a fleece throw around his body and lost himself in his mind, in the permanent files that he kept organized in his head, going over everything mentally, one-by-one, until something new would come to his attention, something that stuck out above the rest. It seemed that no matter how many times he and Rebecca had gone over the files, the best ones were always kept fresh in his mind.

It was still quite early. Normally by this time Rebecca would be strapping on her gun belt and heading in the car to work with Jack, but normalcy didn't exist for this day. Today was a winter emergency. Today not a single soul drove on these streets, and no one would be able to drive anything but a snowmobile for at least a week, maybe longer. Jack couldn't remember a storm this bad before; *even the infamous Blizzard of '76 wasn't this bad*, he thought. Yeah, stores closed down, cops were on snowmobiles and tractors, but the snow never reached this high. Snow never reached the point of burying everyone alive in their homes. Thinking this was just thinking foolishly. That would never happen. Jack knew that without doubt, but the thought, the wonder would linger in his head.

In the den he kept a small twenty-four inch television that sat on a small table adjacent the fireplace. He fumbled between the cushions for the remote control, found it, and turned it on. It was one morning talk show after another, then a news station came on with an alert for another treacherous snowstorm in Central Massachusetts and parts of Southern New Hampshire. *Here comes that buried alive thing.*

They were calling for another two feet by midday tomorrow. Another storm meant more time trapped in his own home. It was beginning to look like an icebox with the windows caked with ice and snow; it felt like a prison. There was no escape but to dig a tunnel out into snowland. *That's what this place should be called – Snowland*, Jack thought to himself.

He finally shut off the television, hid the remote back underneath one of the armrests, and sat still, breathing silently as if to calm himself from a panic attack he was not quite having. "Thank God I'm not claustrophobic," he whispered.

In his mental images, he kept staring at the manager to the Snow Hill Country Club. Something was odd about the fellow, something seemed misplaced; not that he was hiding something, but that *he* was a lie. His answers seemed almost rehearsed for a big Hollywood production of whodunit.

Jack saw other images in his mind, people back as far as from his youth and as recent as meeting Kyle and Kennedy. One woman stood out in his mind. Jacqueline Marquette. She had been arrested for conspiracy to commit murder against her husband for a half-million dollar life insurance policy. That was five-hundred thousand reasons that she'd wanted him dead. The hit man she hired was caught, then testified against her to knock four years off his sentence. She was tall and attractive, though not beautiful. Her face had seen too much of life and was too full of greed, hatred and jealousy to have been beautiful. That was two years ago. The case was closed. And just like the dozens before and the dozens that would come after, each case remained fresh in Jack's memory as if it were on some computer hard drive directly linked to his brain where all these images and documents were stored and organized. He always thought of himself as an elephant, even at a younger age. His grandfather would always smile and say, "You've got the mind of an elephant, young man." Those words struck true to him.

He waited another hour before he heard the familiar footsteps of Rebecca coming down the stairs—or was it Kennedy?

They were light and elegant, carefully placed steps.

Kennedy walked into the den. She looked at Jack as if he would automatically know by the expression on her face that something was wrong. Maybe he did and just refused to believe it himself.

"What's wrong?"

"He's gone," she confessed in sounds of worry. "I can't find him anywhere."

"What do you mean he's gone?" Jack sprung up and rushed out of the bedroom, tailed by Kennedy.

He searched the spare bedroom, the upstairs bathroom, and even the linen closet; every nook and cranny to prove to himself that this was no hoax, that Kyle had really upped and left.

He searched through his downstairs office, hoping that the first thought that came to his mind was just an overreaction. In his desk drawer, his extra gun was missing. It was a shiny .45 that he kept underneath a stack of financial records and a box of pens.

Some of his papers were disorganized, skewed from how he remembered he had left them the day before. *He found it. Sonofabitch!*

The kid was a senior in high school, not a renegade lawman in the Wild West. He'd get himself hurt—or worse, killed.

The papers that were unevenly scattered were take-home notes from the investigation. And "SNOW HILL COUNTRY CLUB" was written in large letters and underlined numerous times. *That's where he must be going.*

On the papers were a list of employee names, Jack's thoughts about each individual, and a whole list that theorists would like to chew up—and Kyle had fed on it like a wild dog feasting on a pig.

"Rebecca," Jack yelled from downstairs, "we need to go."

"What's going to happen?" Kennedy asked frantically.

"I don't know but I think I know where he went," he told her, against his better judgment. He rushed to the window and peered out with his eagle-eyes but couldn't see anything but the solitude of white snow.

"I have to go get him," he said softly, then turned to Kennedy. "Did he say anything to you?"

"No. I just woke up."

"No idea where he was heading, what he was thinking?"

"No."

"Tell me the truth!"

"I am," she shouted back.

Kennedy didn't bother to finish the interrogation; instead she ran back to the bedroom, scared and crying.

Jack thought hard to himself and silently called himself the biggest asshole to ever walk the face of the planet.

What the hell would he expect someone like Kyle to do?

A cop knocks on your door, tells you your parents are deceased, and invites you into a strange home to spend a few days or a few weeks during one of the worst snow storms ever. Now Kyle had gone in search of some rough justice. The streets were empty of all travelers, save for one hard-headed bastard who had stolen a gun and was looking for someone to point it at.

Jack sat down in his armchair by his desk, trying to relax. He knew he should try to calm Kennedy down, but his pride stood in the way of apologies now and again.

He picked up the corded phone on the desk. The lines were still down.

Jack looked at the scattered papers. He stood up, moved to the small closet in the back of the room near the tall filing cabinet, and pulled out a safe that sat on top of a high built-in shelf. He fished for a set of keys from his pocket and unlocked the safe. The contents: a Glock 17 and three full clips. He took the gun, loaded one clip in the handle, and pulled the cylinder back. The click and motion of the barrel was familiar. He placed the weapon and the extra ammo on the desk until he could get properly suited.

# XIII

January 25th, 2009 09:34A.M.

He didn't answer his calls.

Kennedy tried his cell phone at least a couple dozen times, but all of them had the same result: no answer. Kyle had either turned the phone off or he was blatantly ignoring it; hell, maybe he just gave it a good heave into the snow, allowing the hidden computer chips to get soaked and disable the device once and for all.

Kennedy had the feeling of overwhelming dread, as if she knew for a fact that Kyle wouldn't be coming back, thus leaving her utterly alone in this world. With her parents she always felt alone, but with Kyle she had meaning. She believed in herself; she understood her place in life, in his life. She had already accepted that her parents were gone, and she felt bad that she *didn't* feel bad enough. Now she felt heartache for the first time in her life. Maybe it was because Kyle was always there to save the day. *Let's face it*, Kennedy thought. She was a poster girl for abused children everywhere. She got hit, but the verbal abuse was the worst; it played a psychological toll on her, causing her to doubt herself, to question everything she ever knew.

She hadn't done this in a while. She didn't even know if she remembered how to—and she only did this when times got really rough, rarely when they were good.

In the bedroom at the top of the stairs, she fell to her knees and prayed. Prayed to Him, to God, to whoever would be willing to listen. She asked Him to bring Kyle back safely, to bring this whole ordeal to a close. And whether or not anyone would be listening to her whispered prayers, she felt a little better asking for help from a more powerful being.

The windows rattled.

The blowing wind shrieked like a rabid wolf growling and hissing.

The window cracked into a spider web, then shattered with an explosion of glistening glass.

She screamed, short and loud. She collapsed to her butt and peddled herself back toward the wall. The first thought that entered her mind was that coal black creature, that enormous head and anaconda-like tail.

Jack just didn't seem to believe her or Rebecca. And as Kennedy thought about it more and more, she wouldn't have believed such a creature existed had she not seen it with her own eyes.

She stared through the broken window, feeling the cold air rush its way through, depleting any heat the room had occupied. She was too scared to look out the window, too afraid that this *thing* with the huge razor-sharp claws would stick them through her chest and fling her around like she weighed nothing more than a doll you could buy at a toy store on clearance for five bucks with its hair made from cheap string. She imagined herself flailing to death—a white death in the snow.

She had heard rumors from a long time ago about a place an hour outside of Snow Hill—Sinisar, Massachusetts, just on the outskirts of Auburn, in the woods near I-290. Something paranormal had happened there, and something—maybe something similar—was happening here.

In the wake of the late morning, something flashed across Kennedy's mind:

*It was dark and murky.*

*A basement.*

*It was hot and humid, like an eighteenth-century underground prison. She was alone. It was silent. Hieroglyphics lined the walls on either side. It looked like pictures of man and beast, the same beast that attacked her in Jack and Rebecca's home but it was a bit skewed from the original monster. Of course this was painted on concrete and rock, painted in a sculpted image of the real beast. Kennedy was walking around freely, walking a distance that the bedroom did not allow. She felt the rough edges of the stones and smelled a distasteful odor — an odor of death.*

*Down the poorly lit hall, many rooms awaited exploring. The door to each room was almost identical with its rotted hinges and mildew-looking doors with either damaged doorknobs or cracked wood lining the center of it, making it almost effortless to break in.*

*On the walls she saw pictures of clouds with crisscrossed icons that may represent snow, perhaps the name of the city. She had a riptide of intentions to go barreling through each door as if she were invincible, searching through the darkness in the hopes that Kyle would be waiting behind one of those doors. She knew it was silly. This is only some sort of dream.*

*Was she going crazy? Finally losing it?*

*She hoped not.*

*But she continued on, sneaking through shadows, listening for any movement up ahead or behind her, but it was utterly silent save for her own labored breathing. She was hoping not to have a panic attack, but she could tell that one was coming on. It would tighten her chest and make it difficult to breathe, make her legs feel like Jell-o and cause her to collapse to the cold hard cement — or would there be a wooden floor instead?*

"Kennedy, listen, I'm—" Jack walked in and found her staring blankly at the wall, standing only a few inches away from the molding. "Kennedy?" Jack walked closer. This time he spoke louder. "Kennedy?"

Her eyes blinked rapidly out of her trance. She looked around the room, confused and in shock.

"Where was I?"

"What do you mean?" Jack replied.

"I wasn't here a minute ago. I was in a basement or a dungeon. There were so many doors, and that smell—stench like people rotting. Oh God, is that what my parents are going through? Tears welled up in her eyes with the mere thought.

He rushed closer to her, wrapped his arms around her, and told her it'd be all right. He explained to her that that was not quite the way it happened at the medical examiner's office. He didn't bother to go into full details about the Y-incision in the chest, the removal and weighing of organs, the examination of bile fluids. All those details would be too much for a young girl like Kennedy who was all ready in a very fragile state of mind, and he didn't want to be the cause of her going overboard and ending up in the psych ward talking to the walls of a padded room while she was monitored by surveillance cameras for a suicide watch. That was no life to live. Jack had seen it once or twice and had heard enough stories about it to not wish anyone to go through that, not even the worst criminals he'd put behind bars—well, maybe one or two of the nasty ones, like this pedophile he caught a couple of summers ago when he was just walking by the park.

He had seen a twinge in the man's eyes and knew something was about to happen. Luckily, no matter where he went he carried his gun and a set of cuffs in his pocket and his badge secured on a chain around his neck. He had them even on his days off; that badge, gun, and cuffs were like a second skin to him, he never took them off.

Meanwhile, Kennedy stood there trapped in guilt and conflict. She knew Jack was about to give her a speech about his aggravations and Kyle's wrongdoings and apologize to her, but she could care less. All she wanted was Kyle back there with her, to feel that sense of security she got every time she looked into his eyes. She needed that most of all.

She concentrated on her vision, but like a bad dream, it had faded away and left Kennedy without the slightest recollection of her walk through in the basement of Hell—at least, it might as well have been Hell with the thick, humid air and the smell of rotting corpses lingering like lilacs on a spring morning.

"Are you okay?"

"I don't know," she confessed. "I just had—I don't know. It was so real."

"Why don't you lie down," Jack suggested.

Like a little girl, she covered herself up in the blankets just past her chin, as if she were afraid the boogeyman was coming for her and she wanted to be ready at a moment's notice to throw all the sheets over her head for protection.

Nothing could protect her any more.

Jack left the room without the long speech and apologetic contortion. He had bigger things to do, like finding Kyle in the heap of the snowland that had built up outside over the past few days.

Jack went into his office. He looked through a few desk drawers and found a little silver key. In the back of a small closet were he kept his coats and old sweaters he also kept a small safe. He placed the key firmly in the hole and twisted the black metal handle. The door opened. He pulled out a grey case about the size of a laptop bag only thinner. He carried it by its handle and placed it on his desk on top of the scattered paperwork. He fumbled for the combination in the middle of the case and it snapped opened, revealing two Glock 17s and two clips filled with ammo, snug in their microfiber cushion.

He had to find Kyle before he got his ass killed.

Jack had the law to protect; he had to do things by the book. He needed to call his CO, call for backup if any were riding around on snowmobiles. And right about then, Jack was thinking that the rules he was forced to play by were really fucking overrated.

# XIV

January 25th, 2009 11:04A.M.

He had no idea how he had made it here. It was a combination of pure will, untainted desire and determination to beat the odds.

The doors to the facility were nearly covered by the snow save for a few inches of the upper door frame. He would need to get in through one of the windows on the second floor. He didn't want to smash it in, rattle up a storm inside, and call attention to himself, but he saw no other alternative. He grabbed the gun from his waistband and crashed the butt of the gun through the window. He stayed close to the side of the building in case someone was alerted to his forced entry.

He stood there calmly, able to control his breathing with nice thoughts, gentle thoughts about making it out of here and getting to someplace warm, to see Kennedy again, to see Shadow.

A heavy gust of wind shook loose icicles that had been dangling from the rooftop. They landed near Kyle's feet—thank God none of them had hit him or he could have easily been impaled by one of those bastards. Though nothing would surprise him, not any more. Fiendish ghouls could come tailgating out of the walls looking to slice and dice him with razor-sharp arm-swords and that wouldn't rate too high on his Holy Fuck Barometer. Not after seeing what he'd seen; not after seeing an entire city crippled by snow. And who knows how many innocent people were on the road when this shit-weather took its toll, how many fatalities there were brought on by cars running into one another or off the road into a ditch, being buried and suffocating in a frozen tomb. There was no way to tell. And Kyle certainly did not want to be added to that statistic.

He wait just another moment, trying to make sure he heard no footsteps at all—but could he be totally sure over the sound of the howling wind whipping through the eaves?

He took his chances and crawled in.

Kyle found himself in a bedroom. *Do country clubs have bedrooms? Or is this where the cheap hookers come to earn a paycheck?*

The room was just an ordinary room. It had a dresser and mirror, a queen-size bed, and like-new carpeting. It looked as if the person who lived here was very tidy. He found the light switch on the far wall across from the broken window. He flipped it on, then off and on again. It didn't work. The light from the snow shined in well enough to see his footsteps and about five feet in front of him, but not much more.

The clouds were closing in. They were getting darker, colder. It was like a bad dream: rolling clouds of ash absorbing the city, shrouding everything good and proper.

Out into the long, narrow hallway it was quiet and eerie.

Flashes of lightning bounced within the darkening clouds. *Oh, shit! This must be one hell of a storm.* Kyle had never known for a lightning storm to hit in the dead of winter—but this winter was very much alive and kicking.

He gripped the handle of the gun, its smooth, cold handle fitting just right around his fingers and his palm; feeling its weight and adjusting appropriately, ready to aim it at any poor son of a bitch that dared to come after him. And he'd shoot, too! Oh, he'd fire the whole fucking clip off if he had to, then he'd wing it at the fucker just to add insult to injury. Yeah. He'd do that.

He walked carefully and cautiously down the long stretch of hallway, placing his ear up to each door for a moment to listen in, but all the rooms seemed to be vacant. He walked down the carpeted steps to the first floor and found another staircase that wrapped around in a spiral, leading toward the basement.

He walked slowly down the steps. It was cold. A ruffled breeze blew in from the cracks in the foundation. It was dark, with only the hint of light coming through. He could make out the pictures that lined the walls with such grace and performance, something he would have seen in National Geographic. He didn't bother to look closely at the pictures or try to decipher their meanings. He was too busy wondering where they hell he was. Kyle had seen weird a few times over, but this really cut the cake. This bizarre, unnatural place undoubtedly beat any novel or movie he had ever seen. It gave him a quick chill and a sudden awareness that he was utterly alone, with nothing but seventeen bullets to protect himself.

Further on the hall, he heard someone, and from deep within the darkness he saw figures silhouetted from beyond this midnight hallway.

He stuck close to the walls, keeping out of sight, and crept carefully closer to the voices. They were speaking a different language, something he couldn't understand. It wasn't French or Spanish, he knew that much.

A crack in the gloom opened up. Through an open room on the left, he saw several lit windows like wide eyes staring back at him, judging him.

The voices still carried on farther away. A rapid flush of terror raced across his spine and his heart cracked against his ribs. He gripped the gun tighter, feeling the grooves, making it one with his hand and holding it out, lining up the sight with his eye, ready to blow someone's ass to oblivion.

He waited, listening for the footsteps, but they went away.

The basement hall must have stretched a couple hundred yards with several turnoffs and rooms to enter like a multilayered dungeon in the lowest depths of Hell. But no prisoners were kept here. No chains rattled. No starving, unkept men were wandering around like slaves trying to spare themselves from death. This was something new. Different.

He walked the halls like a lost puppy, swaying from side to side, looking for something to catch his attention—perhaps some sort of means to salvation or a chance to find and wipe out his parents' murderer. That's why he was here after all, that's why he'd snuck out of the house with one of Jack's guns. He had no intention of listening to reason from the person who cut the brake line to the car his parents were driving on that lonely road. He was going to aim for the chest, and squeeze the trigger until all the bullets were let out of the chamber. He was looking for revenge. Not justice.

His parents' murderer had shown no justice.

You can bet your ass that he'd return the favor in full.

Kyle rubbed his hands against the wall, brushing off dust. He sneezed. The engravings didn't look man-made. They were too perfect. He supposed a high-tech machine could've done the job right. Isn't that what they had billion-dollar companies do? Make machines to do things in a perfect motion that man could not quite get the handle on yet?

Kyle could tell right off the bat that Jack and Rebecca were both good at their job, two hard-edged cops trying to make a difference in the world—if only they knew what he was up to. And by now they had to. Jack had to have noticed his gun missing, had to notice Kyle was up and gone, climbing over every snow bank and ice mound until he reached the Snow Hill Country Club. And like Jack wrote down in his notes, there was something strange about this place. Not that average strange feeling you get when you enter someplace new. Not that same smell where you can't quite tell if it's a new carpet or cleaning supplies. This was just the plain ole fuck-ya-in-the-ass strange.

The first room he visited had a slew of plants as if it were an office and the occupant got too many unoriginals for decoration.

The next several rooms were bare. They had a broken-concrete structure to them as if they were only kept for storage rooms, but they had not been filled yet save for the creepy-crawlers in the corners scattering about over one another, like maggots slithering their white bodies near rotted food.

This place was full of mystery, and the more rooms Kyle entered the more it seemed like one big jigsaw puzzle with too many missing pieces to make the picture come out clear enough. From within the shadows he felt as though he was being watched, though shining the flashlight over to the right and to the left like a light show proved that he was the only one wandering through this hall. But the feeling never left. To him, this was a haunted house fable with a slight twist of a who's-who.

He heard a noise coming from the far end of the hall. It looked like the hall stretched on forever; it was just an endless hall full of only God-knows-what.

On the rare occasion of need, he prayed. This was such a time. He didn't kneel or bow his head, he just spoke softly in his mind. And doing so seemed to calm him. Kyle's heart, which had been beating like a jackhammer, simmered down. The sweat that had protruded down his brow stopped in a cold hesitation. He wondered that if he didn't come back, would he be able to talk to God? Would there be a bright white light where he'd be going or would he fade into the dark abyss?

Kyle opened his mouth to snap a retort out, but his fear froze him silent.

He wasn't alone.

Something reached out for him in the shadows, grabbed his arm, and knocked the flashlight loose from his grip. The gun went off. Two rounds and a puff of smoke gnarled lazily in the air. The gun clanked to the ground.

A figure emerged from the shadows, frantic from the gunfire.

Kyle was flailing his arms around as if to take on an army of assailants.

But it was only a girl.

"I didn't mean to scare you," she said shyly. "Please don't hurt me."

"You didn't—I won't."

"I need your help," she begged. "I need to get out of this hell."

The girl was in her late teens and scrawny. She looked like a complete mess. Worse than just a mean futile expression of hopelessness or a girl lost. Her tanned skin was darkened by dirt and soot. Her black hair was frizzled and she looked like she hadn't had a good night's sleep in weeks. Her clothes were bland and worn, like a prisoner's jumpsuit; grey with a barcode over her left breast.

"Who are you?" Kyle asked.

"Chelsea."

"I'm Kyle. What the hell are you doing here?"

"I don't know. I'm payment."

"What?"

"That's what my parents called me. They said I'd be payment so they could stay for the transformation. I don't even know what it all means," she cried. "I was brought down here a few months ago before the blizzards started. I've been trapped here ever since."

Kyle could see a light in her eyes, a gleam of sincerity and hopefulness. She was held captive here and now it was about time she be freed.

"I came here to get the motherfuckers who murdered my parents," he told her angrily, reaching down for Jack's gun.

"You don't want to do that," she warned him. "They'll kill you. They killed just about everyone else here, except for me, I guess."

"What do you mean?"

"They kill kids. I've seen kids come and go for the past three months. There was Cody, he was seven years old, the youngest I've seen here. He was the first. I was the oldest prisoner, so I might've been left for last."

He stared at her in awe, wondering if what he was hearing was really true.

"We have to get out of here," she told him.

"I just came through the window in one of the rooms down the hall," Kyle said. "Just go out the same way I came, over the snow. Go get some help, go to the hospital or police station."

"You don't know…"

"Know what?"

Chelsea took him by the hand and walked him down the hall. "Which room?" she asked.

Kyle pointed as they walked in. She led him back to the shattered window and suggested that he look out it.

When he did, his stomach twisted in knots, his head began to spin all wobbly like a drunken man. The bed that occupied the room was in the perfect position when Kyle's legs went numb. He collapsed onto the cushioned springs, the gun slipping loose from his hand and his eyes rolling back into his head as his body shut down. His breathing was hard and heavy, even in his unconscious state.

Moments later his eyes flashed opened. He grabbed onto his surroundings hard and mean. He panicked. For a slight second he forgot where he was and how he got there. For a slight moment he forgot that Chelsea was looking over him almost in awe, wondering when he would return. It only took a few seconds, but to Kyle it might have been a few days. To put it mildly, he was overwhelmed.

Chelsea held the gun now, but she posed no threat. She placed it on the bed by his side and sat down next to him.

"Are you okay?"

"I don't know — I don't know what the fuck is going on," he told her. "Everything is different, everything has changed."

"I know."

"What's outside?"

"A place you don't want to go. This isn't like our world, it's another world or dimension or another planet. I don't fully understand, either. I never did until one night I heard my parents talking in their bedroom, the night before my little brother went missing."

"Missing?" He said it for the sake of saying it, but knew almost instinctively what she meant. Her brother never went *missing*, he was taken.

"I never knew what had happened to him. That was about fourteen months ago, and then I saw him in here. He was six years younger than me, so they took him first."

"What happened?" Kyle didn't want to know the answer, but he was compelled to ask.

"He's most likely dead now." Her lips cringed, her chin quivered.

Chelsea helped Kyle off the bed, her hair caressing her face like a savage beast, wild and firm almost in a lustrous surge. The lights in the hall flickered brighter.

They heard footsteps.

The shafts of light expanded, spilling in the room. They hid in the confines of the shadows.

The footsteps were almost animalistic, stepping heavy and fast, purposefully. One of the doors jostled loose, opening up into the oddly depths of a prison cell. And from several yards away, a man cursed and slammed the door. He was at Chelsea's room. She had escaped, but he knew she hadn't traveled too far away from her captivity chamber. By the speedy footsteps, Kyle and Chelsea could tell the man was hurrying away to alert someone.

Kyle still couldn't believe what he saw outside.

When he had came sloshing through the snow it was daylight, now it was dusk with a heavy thick layer of fog, surrounding everything in whole, swallowing every dwelling and road sign and street lamp. It was like Snow Hill no longer existed outside. The snow was still there, thunder and lightning still displayed its wrath, and a coat of fog wrapped itself around the Snow Hill Country Club. It was like all the elements were being abused by a greater force than Mother Nature.

Kennedy stayed fresh in Kyle's mind, and he wondered if he'd ever see her again; wondered if he'd ever play with Shadow again; thinking what if he never made it out of there.

The outside world was gone. Now all that remained was the inside of a nut-job factory.

The same familiar footsteps returned. Kyle and Chelsea held their breath; Kyle readied his weapon and crept closer to the door. He heard a loud banging noise, as if someone was trying to hang a picture on the wall. The side of hammer on nail makes a distinct sound, a sound that Kyle was somewhat familiar with. Then the sound was replaced by a *squish* and the footsteps went away.

They waited several minutes to see if they heard the footsteps of the cursing man again, but he did not return. When they entered the hallway again, Chelsea backed up, her hands covering her mouth in utter shock; Kyle stood in pure horror at the sight of a child no older than thirteen hung on the wall by a two-foot spike through his back and protruding through his chest. He was dead, badly beaten and bruised; he had been knifed or blundered in a scuffle; crusty slashes streaked across his naked body; a broken arm hung loose like a damaged branch.

Kyle quickly grabbed Chelsea and pulled her close to him, shielding her face from the scene.

"That's Billy," she cried out. She said something else, but it was unintelligible through the sobs.

It was her brother.

"See what they do!" She pounded at his chest. "She what they do here!" She cried again, her tears waving in brown rivers, cleaning the dirt from her face.

"It'll be okay," he told her, not even sure if he believed it himself. It was one of those false hopes you tell someone when they've lost someone dear to them.

Footsteps grew closer. Not just one set, but many, marching in a rhythmic beat from the far end of the hall. Chelsea wiped her eyes, grabbed Kyle's hand, and rushed out of the room toward her secret hiding spot.

They were followed.

# XV

January 29th, 2009 9:37P.M.

Thursday evening the house was still and quiet.

The snow had began to melt, thankfully, and the people in Snow Hill were getting back to normal. Everyone but Jack, Rebecca, and Kennedy. Being a cop prepares you for certain things like finding a missing child dead or interviewing a rape victim, but it never equipped Jack and Rebecca to deal with Kyle's disappearance. Over eighteen inches of snow had melted away and certain vehicles could access the roads again. Jack called the station to have one of the SUVs pick them up. They were going back to Jack's original hunch, to Kyle's possible whereabouts.

These past four days, Kennedy had been locked up in her room crying, avoiding Jack and Rebecca as best as she could. It was in her stubbornness that she pleaded with them to let her go look for Kyle; to look for him in the streets, to have the police helicopter search for him. She thought of a hundred different ways to go about it, but they held her back, especially from going outside to look for him herself.

She wasn't really mad at them. She knew it was impossible to do most of the things she suggested, and the things that were possible were still unsafe. She understood their reasoning, but to her it felt as though they couldn't understand *her*. Kyle was all she had left in this world and it seemed like they were giving up without trying first.

Kennedy had been wrapped up in a blanket for hours, staring out the bedroom window, making little breaks for the bathroom but not much else, not even to eat. Every so often, she'd go to the bathroom, cup her hand under the faucet, and drink cold tap water which seemed to just hit the spot when she was thirsty enough.

***

Today Jack was going to look for Kyle. He was packing enough ammo to start a war in a third-world country. He was *Rambo* or *G.I. Joe*—whatever nickname that involved big guns, lots of ammo, and a tough *sonofabitch*; that was him, or at least for today it was.

Rebecca grabbed her gear, too.

The marked SUV would be there in a few moments.

Rebecca felt bad for not being there for Kennedy like Jack was for her when she got that news so long ago in college. She could either console her or find Kyle and bring him home. She chose the latter. And to her surprise, Kennedy hadn't even bothered to ask to tag along. Of course they would have told her no, but now it seemed like she had given up.

Rebecca remained wholly still and silent for a brief moment, mentally replaying what she'd like to happen and how she wanted the events to take place. She knew the odds were overwhelmingly not in their favor and there was only one thing left to do: find Kyle. Hopefully before anything happened to him.

Jack felt high, as if he were on drugs. Adrenaline was as good as speed; it made your heart race, it felt good flowing through your system, making you feel invincible, as if you could singlehandedly take on an army.

The temperature outside was in the high fifties. It brought with it a cool dank chill that rustled through the eaves and rattled the windows as it howled outside like a vicious predator.

Kennedy stayed in her room. She didn't move; barely took a breath. It was like she was in a comatose state. She missed Kyle.

*Joseph McGee*

# XVI

January 29th, 2009 9:55P.M.

Kyle was hiding in the wall.

It was dark there. He stayed close to Chelsea, held her hand. And at night, when it got cold, they would wrap their bodies together to stay warm. No one knew where they were. This was Chelsea's hiding place. She kept seeing the image of her brother over and over again in her mind; hanging there, naked. He never stood a chance. *Those pricks*, she thought. How could anyone do that to their own child?

After what he was told by Chelsea four days before, he had nearly had another panic attack and fainted. She explained to him everything she knew about this place, about what she found downstairs in one of the sub-basement levels. Number 6, she thought it was. Had to have been. Level 7 required some type of special clearance that she couldn't get or forge. In all her time there, Level 7 was never mentioned. It was beginning to seem more and more like a government facility than a country club. It seemed like a thousand different fantasies—mostly violent and absurd.

Kyle didn't know where he was, but he sure as hell knew he wasn't in Kansas anymore.

Footsteps echoed in the hall.

They—whoever they were—had begun a four-day search for "the eldest," as they called her. The broken window had been found and a search had begun outside, though they never thought she could have survived it—and they were right. She knew she wouldn't have been able to survive the bitter cold or this world she stood on, period.

They had no food and only the very little water they managed to get from the moisture that had built up near the broken window. They had mastered a makeshift plan of escape — or exploration — down into the pit of the facility.

*Another fucking day in paradise*, Kyle thought.

They crawled out of the small boarded-up hole that didn't seem like a small infant could fit through. The men had left. Most of them were outside searching in the snow banks, wearing snowshoes so they wouldn't crumble to the bottom of one of the mounds. Kyle wondered how far it was to the surface beneath all the snow.

With their white camouflage suits and guns and ski masks, these men looked like soldiers, like they were a special ops unit from the military. This wasn't a Tom Clancy novel, but it sure as hell felt like one.

The sun never set, nor had it ever risen into the Great Beyond outside. It was as dark as midnight on a country road. No one had closed in the window with plywood yet, and there was no way to tell if they ever planned to. It'd be a good plan B escape route if the case ever called for such a drastic measure as jumping out of a window onto feet-upon-feet of snow, painfully freezing off asses and perking up nipples.

Kyle and Chelsea made their way down to the opposite end of the hall. As they descended the circular staircase Kyle's stomach tightened. For a moment, he felt not himself; he felt like a hero in a movie saving the damsel in distress. He tried hard to force himself into reality mode, to get back inside his body and simply find a way out, not a way deeper into the cavity of Hell. The stairs were metal and bolted to a small shaft that couldn't be much wider than five feet. It was just enough to house the staircase and the few lights that were stuck to the wall on the way down. They were brass sconces that looked antique, or just brushed copper that someone had found at the hardware store to make them look like they were antiques.

The further they went the colder it got.

They hugged the walls and kept to the shadows all the way down, peering around cautiously as they continued toward the eerie white glow at the bottom. There was no one in sight. At the bottom was a small room, about eight feet-by-eight feet. Words were written on the wall, but they weren't in English. It was something else. Kyle thought it might have been Greek. He remembered a textbook on Greek mythology he had been forced to read, courtesy of his tenth grade class.

In a brown bowl sat seven marbles, all different colors. Beside it to the right was a wooden bar with seven equally spread out holes.

Στην ευθυγράμμιση πρέπει να είναι.

He couldn't read it. But he could tell the seven marbles must be lined up together in a certain order. Seeing the colors brought him back to his fifth grade science fair project, a model of the solar system. But there were nine planets, not seven. He looked at them again, took the marbles in his hand. *God forgive me if I'm wrong.*

"What are you doing?"

"I don't know," Kyle admitted. "Just hold on. Don't say a word."

One-by-one he placed them in the holes. First an orange-red that might've represented the sun. He placed that in the fourth slot. Then he put the marbles in the slots corresponding to Earth, Mars and Neptune. On the left, he placed Mercury, Venus, and Jupiter.

A loud, echoing click rattled the walls. The concrete block slid aside allowing entrance.

"Holy shit. I can't believe I was right." He smiled, then nervously laughed. It was almost a lunatic's laugh. He grabbed her hand and walked through.

The door closed tightly behind them, silent until it clicked back into place — then it was too late.

They had entered a long, wide room leading to other rooms. Flickering fire jumped out from torches on the walls. They were the sole means of light in this tomb. As they got closer, Kyle and Chelsea saw buttons and engraved words above each and every doorknob. There were no keyholes, just buttons that might open the doors; for all they knew, it could call security with loud sirens and flashing red lights.

Kyle felt a strong gust of air caress his face as if someone had opened an air-compressed room. It was frigid in there; it had to be in the forties or below. Neither of them wore anything that resembled a heavy coat. Kyle had taken his off upstairs when hiding between slabs of sheetrock, where it was confined and felt hard to breath. He had fought the urge to strip down to his bare skin so his body could breath better, could feel every subtle breeze that blew by from the broken open window, which were too rare to begin with.

"Where do we go?" Chelsea asked, her white teeth sticking out more than usual on her unclean face.

"I don't know."

It was a simple answer. It was the truth. It was an endless hallway like a prison, each side lined with doors. And there was no end in sight. It was too dark to see anything substantial in the dimness.

In her mind, Chelsea thought of her brother being kept down here in this horrible dungeon; the others, too. She wondered which cell was his and if there were any more kids locked up, marked next in line for a horrible death.

The doors were solid steel. A small rectangular slit allowed viewing into each cell. Most of them were vacant, at least the first dozen they looked in.

The gun imprinted the handle crest into Kyle's back, almost fusing him and the gun together. He drew it out and pointed it downward. He tightened his grip around it like he was choking his parents' killer, hard and relentless; muscles pushing out, tension reading on his trigger finger.

He was ready to kill.

Kyle could feel it in his veins. He wanted revenge. He was ready to shoot at anything human that posed a threat to him or Chelsea. Doubts crossed his mind about his newfound friend. *Why was she spared? Was she in on it, too?* He knew better than that. She had had the past few days to kill him if that was her intent. But he kept looking over his shoulder at her, allowing paranoia to weigh in. She squeezed his left hand for reassurance. Kyle would have liked to believe that she was holding his hand tightly for her own sake, but it was also to comfort him.

The smog that shrouded the room evaporated the further they went on. The next section was separated by a half-open door. There the letter B was written in blood-red on the right side of the wall.

"They must be broken up into sections," Kyle thought out loud.

Chelsea grabbed on to the wall to help her walk, like a crutch. She stuck her palm to it, using Kyle and the wall as guidance, as if she were a blind woman. Yet a strong sense of familiarity overcame her. She had never been to this freezing rattrap on the bottom level, but somehow everything looked like she had seen it before, like a living area in her home — before her parents had sold their children to evil. Her poor brother had been hung in the middle of the upper rooms, so they *had* to have known her whereabouts, yet they did nothing but start an outside sweep, thinking she had left to find sanctuary beyond the perimeter. She couldn't tell if they had cameras sticking in the walls. Some were so small nowadays they could be anywhere and feedback to a million widescreen televisions close by or on the other side of the world. She wasn't stupid, just paranoid, which had started on the day she found out what her parents had done. What was so important, so great to sell your children for it? To give them up, to purposely put them in harm's way—what was so desirable? Moms and dads all across the globe abandoned their children, beat on them just because it was Thursday, and she'd rather take that than knowing that they who provided love and affection, took her to the zoo, to the park, to Disney World had given her up for something she couldn't even understand, something that was so far gone she didn't even know if she'd ever find out the truth. And the only thing that was allowing her to walk around, to have some shy glimpse of hope, was a stranger not much older than herself carrying a handgun for protection that he had stolen from a cop. And if she ever made it out of this life, back to her own home, back into a soft comfortable bed, she'd thank him in a million ways; she might even turn tricks in the bedroom for him if he could manage to rescue her from this hellhole.

Kyle's thoughts were on everything but what Chelsea would do for him if he saved her. His eyes stared straight ahead like laser beams in the night, locking his sight like a damn robot, while walking the halls of the closest thing to darkness he'd ever known.

Footsteps echoed yards behind them. They froze, listened. It sounded like an army marching their way. Dozens of footsteps all in one rhythmic motion.

They were about to be hunted.

Kyle squeezed Chelsea's hand and pulled her along, running, the loud thumping of Kyle's sneakers and the slosh of Chelsea's feet hitting the smooth steel floor.

The hallway was constructed with sheets of metal, bolted to one another like the inside of a submarine: close quarters, thick steel all around, and not a single slice of daylight to trap in any room.

They ran as fast as they could until they came to an end where the next doorway led to a much larger room, quite possibly larger than a football field. In the center of everything sat an open tank full of water, about fifteen feet in diameter. It seemed the room was surrounded by water, like a giant aquarium. By the looks of it, the pool went underground as well. It seemed like there was something built into the water with thick glass and heavy sheets of steel bolted down tightly. It was an aqua-village.

Something was moving around in the center of the tank, something large; thrashing in the water like a shark, and angry as hell.

The room was lined with wall to wall glass. There must have been thousands of gallons of water surrounding this place; with all sorts of underwater creatures swimming by. Maybe that's where they were, Kyle thought, an underground facility built in the water, perhaps off the coast of Boston Harbor, or maybe Virginia Beach. Neither was too far away. And, as Kyle well knew by then, anything could happen. He wouldn't be surprised if he saw Santa Claus and the Easter Bunny playing poker just yonder, smoking cigars and drinking beer.

The footsteps came closer.

Kyle saw a half-open panel in the back of the tank where the temperature control was. He pushed it open all the way. There was only room for one. Without a word, he shoved Chelsea into the small cupboard and gestured for her to be quiet.

They were closing in.

Kyle did the only thing he could do. He grabbed on tightly to the gun, clenched the brim of the tank that stood just about as tall as he was, and jumped in, holding his breath in midair, not worrying about whatever underwater animal lurked about in the murky water.

Diving in, he felt fins graze his legs and swim off into the unknown. He was careful not to get sucked in any deeper, to lose his sense of awareness for where he was and ultimately drown in the process.

The men in uniform searched the aquarium high and low, checking every possible hiding place, except for inside the control panel. They shined their lights on every dark corner, behind every obstruction that would give shelter for the two wanted kids. Then they went further down and out of sight. They were trained for this sort of thing; carrying their guns with the stock held tightly to their shoulder, raised at eye level for the perfect kill. These men were predators, trained by some branch of the government or some rogue outfit that had unknown intentions, which even the soldiers wouldn't know of. That's how it worked. The men who did the killing were just following commands; it's the ones who are in charge that know the evil deeds committed by these puppets with skillful backgrounds and large guns.

Kyle floated to the top of the tank, only revealing part of his face for a gasp of air. Silently he took in a lungful, and once again held his breath and pushed himself underneath, trying to wait them out.

He forced his eyes shut as tightly as he could to keep the water from burning them. He held his gun, not knowing if it'd shoot underwater or not, but in case a large, man-eating something-or-other came on by, he'd have the chance to put a couple of rounds in its head.

Eventually Kyle couldn't hear the static of their radio frequency any more.

He emerged out of the water, silently, like a Navy SEAL, letting the water wash over his face. He opened his eyes, pushing aside the burning sensation, the kind you get when you're taking a shower and soap gets in your eye. His eyes swelled a bit, then his vision pooled back together again. Whoever they were, they were gone. They'd left to sweep some other end of the compound. For seemingly highly trained operatives, they had missed Kyle and Chelsea from right underneath their noses—or had they? It might have been an elaborate trap to keep them dodging the bullet until they were finally too tired to run any more. Then it would be much easier for them to give up than continue the chase.

Kyle took in all the air he could handle in one serving, drinking it up like a fine Italian wine. He climbed out of the tank soaking wet; his shirt clinging to his body like an extra coat of skin. His pants had gained an extra twenty pounds from the moisture. Kyle began to shiver. The water was at a temperature that you desperately tried to stay away from on a cool spring day. It couldn't be above fifty; the cold air made its way through, feeling like a hundred knifes stabbing at him from every which angle.

This place looked like a fantasy novel come to life. It had all the makings of a bestseller. But this wasn't a fantasy; it wasn't a luxurious daydream. This was something far worse, far too surreal for it to be anything less than a living nightmare.

Kyle peeled back the panel and helped Chelsea out.

"That was close," she said.

"Tell me about it."

"Where do we go next?"

"Lead the way," he pointed down the long, dreary walk through the aquarium.

"I hope we're almost out."

"Likewise," Kyle said.

It came from the tank, reached its long, thick body out, and with an open mouth, crunched down on Chelsea.

She screamed. Her body was ripped and punctured. Blood poured from this reptilian creature's mouth. In a sickening sticky burst of blood, it dragged Chelsea's body into the pool. She fought a losing battle. Kyle grabbed on to her arm, but it tore off, and he dropped it with a nauseating thud as blood poured profusely from the wound.

Chelsea's body was now in bits and pieces, more to the creature's liking. The water quickly turned crimson; Chelsea's face was pressed up against the glass, not breathing, eyes wide open.

Kyle stood back in disbelief. "Jesus Christ!"

He couldn't help her now. Something that looked similar to a whale had snagged her with its razor-sharp teeth and had itself a human treat. The thrashing of the animal caused blood to splash over the brim of the tank; pieces of organs and small body parts fell to the steel floor, splatters of red water colored Kyle's pants as a permanent reminder of Chelsea.

Kyle's eyes were as wide as the horizon sun, his heart felt like a million hammers beating down on it, his stomach tightened, and bile rose to his throat. He bent his knees and vomited a clear and yellow mess.

He fell backwards, looking at the tank, seeing Chelsea's lifeless face stare back at him like nothing was the matter. She looked so innocent. She didn't deserve this. No one did. And Kyle was afraid that it was coming back for him.

He clambered to his feet and ran in the same direction that the military men had gone.

Kyle was in this alone, again.

He ran for a good ten minutes. Just running as fast as his legs would carry him until he needed to stop, to slouch down against one of the walls and take a breather, to give his heart a chance to slow down, to let his mind take everything in. But that was the worst thing he could do—relive what happened to Chelsea. What if that had been Kennedy? *My God, she could've been killed if she had gone with me. What the fuck am I doing here? What the fuck is going on?* He held the gun to his head and wacked himself once, then twice out of frustration. *This cannot be happening. It doesn't make sense. Am I going completely fucking crazy? They might as well lock me in a ten-by-ten padded room at some hospital. This can't be happening. Can it? Is it? My God, what's going on?*

The rants and raves in his head didn't seem to help much to clear his thoughts. Maybe he was going crazy. Maybe sometime soon he would wake up right next to Kennedy and realize that this was all just some horrible dream, a nightmare of which he couldn't awake from until the last piece of the puzzle was solved. And that may be a while. It may take a few more lives in the process, but he'd figure it out, then he'd be the hero. And all of this would go away and be quickly forgotten.

But he knew the truth.

He wasn't going crazy. This was real.

And now, he must face it head on if he ever hoped to get back to the life he left behind in Snow Hill.

The aquarium made a slight right turn, and the sight of the walls he now saw made him vomit again; it made his stomach twist and knot, turn and shuffle. There were dead bodies—naked bodies—stuck right through the abdomen and hanging from hooks. It looked like some grotesque wallpaper. Body parts were missing. On the women, their breasts were cut off their chests, and dribbles of red tears stretched down the women's legs from hanging tissues and organs slipping out from their vaginal area; the men's genitals were hacked off as well. They too bled like rivers down the steel walls and onto the floor, making a thick, sticky pool of blood. Some of them moved and squirmed, and most had permanent lunatic smiles on their faces, as if they had enjoyed it like some sick ritualistic sacrifice.

"Jesus! Are they still alive?" Kyle wondered out loud.

They were. Some were just dying from the loss of too much blood; others were already dead and hanging limp.

Those that were still alive squirmed around, moaning in pain. They were all different; men and women, black and white and Asian and Hispanic. Racism wasn't a factor here. They were eight bodies high and about ten or twelve wide. He had to walk past the blood-stained floor to reach the next room, perhaps the room that contained the key to living in this fucked up place. Then he could go back home and make some weekly appointments with a really good shrink.

The flickering blue-green from the aquarium lights still gave off a glow. It was the only thing to light up the room. Kyle's flashlight had been lost shortly after he had passed out upstairs, after looking out the window at some new, distant world. The gun he still clung to in the back of his waistband had yet to be used, and now he wasn't looking forward to using it. Maybe if Jack and Rebecca knew where he was then he wouldn't have to use it. Jack could come in here and arrest the people responsible for his family's death, and now Chelsea's and her brother's, and the countless others that hung on the wall like trophies.

It was wall-to-wall naked corpses that seemed to be stripped to nothing more than sexless carcasses. Down the middle of the narrow walkway there was a small space to put one foot in front of the other. Kyle carefully walked through, trying to avoid entrails on his sneakers. He made it about twenty yards, then had to make a right turn into a very similar area. It was wider, but contained the same horrific wall ornaments as before.

He heard a woman scream. She was down at the far end, about a football field's length away. There were three men. She was naked. They took a large hatchet, and carved down across her breasts, one at a time. She cried out in agonizing pain, the most horrible cry Kyle had ever heard. Flaps of skin and fatty tissue fell to the ground as a torrent of blood followed. While she was still held by two of them, the third with the knife bent down, peeled her pink clit back, and jabbed her upward, then twisted. She cried again, louder, and then suddenly stopped as the man with the blade fished inside her. Blood rained over the metal, and he retracted the blade from her. She was unable to walk; too scared to talk. They plunged a wooden spike through her stomach, stretching it out, ripping her skin. Her eyes were wide and blood forced its way past her lips. They turned her around, as the others were facing, and bolted her to a copper plating. There were more set up above her; more victims waiting to fall into the hands of this ungodly fate.

Kyle stuck close to the walls, stepping in a hundred people's blood, using their bodies as cover, shielding himself from being seen.

Maybe by now they had found Chelsea's body in the pool and the search would be over. There were no indications that another person had stumbled onto this place, and though he was paranoid, it didn't seem like a place where you'd see cameras pointing at every different angle, not at a human slaughterhouse.

He waited for the three men to go, and waited even longer to make sure another victim would not be hung just yet. The coast was clear. He walked on further, keeping quiet and being cautious. There was no doubt in his mind that he was in some serious shit now, shit so high that he wasn't sure if he'd ever make it out—Chelsea certainly hadn't. He blamed himself for her death. Panic was courting him. But the sense of doubt and rage and uncertainty in his ability to continue on did not strike him down just yet. It was only for the sake of seeing Kennedy again that made him want to make it out alive—what kept him going. Seeking revenge didn't seem worth a dime now. *How many people must die before someone does something about this?* He looked at the walls of death, remembering the last time he had seen his parents alive, remembering the last time he felt Kennedy sleeping next to him, holding on tight for dear life. He remembered how Shadow would wag his tail every time he came home. That kept him strong. That motivated him to get the fuck out of Dodge. It's amazing how simple memories mean the most.

Kyle Johnson had begun the last hours of his life—or the first hours of redemption.

# XVII

January 29th, 2009 10:47P.M.

The lights were down. No one came to the buzzing at the door.

Jack flashed his badge up to the camera, but no one came. The lieutenant had spoken to the captain who had called in a favor to the Assistant District Attorney to get an all-access search warrant to the premises. They were guaranteed to have one ready and signed by the judge before they went in, and a uniformed cop would bring the hard copy of it down for the manager to take witness. They had to do it by the book, to legally search the property without mishap to the investigation. Rebecca and a uniformed cop who drove the SUV sat in the warm interior of the car, waiting for backup to arrive with the warrant.

Jack shouted, pounded on the door, pressed the buzzer a dozen times; he did everything but shoot at the door to get someone's attention.

They were going to have a tactical team come down here to break open the electric lock and sweep the entire building from top to bottom. Jack was going to enjoy this; it was like sex to him, he might even get a stiff one tossing the place and playing hardball with that pencil-necked manager. He was down for the *Dirty Harry* in him now. But now he just waited, shouting at the camera, pounding on the door with a closed fist.

He walked back to the SUV. Rebecca rolled down her window.

"No one's answering. I wonder where…"

"Look!" Rebecca said, pointing at one of the upper windows.

The window was smashed. Jack immediately checked underneath the window for broken glass. There were very few pieces of glass outside, most of which blended right in with the snow.

"It was broken from the outside in," he told her. This might just be proper cause to enter without having the warrant in hand.

Rebecca opened the car door and got out, the cold wind hitting her body furiously. But it was not as bad as last week when the blizzard took control over the entire Northeast. The snow was down to a minimum. It had melted a great deal over these past few days, enough so that cars were able to drive; businesses, although slow, were starting to open back up now, but the schools were still closed, bad for the kids who would have to make it up in the summer.

The window was two stories high; there was no way Jack could shimmy up the wall or find a ladder close by. Jack had a feeling in his gut that this was Kyle's work. He prayed to God that Kyle was still alive and fairing well. He had a gun, and if there was armed security — my God! Jack could just picture Kyle with holes in his body, lying in a pool of his own blood, eyes closed peacefully.

"There's something we've got to do," Jack said.

"Like what? We need to wait for the warrant," Rebecca reminded him.

"Fuck the warrant!" He hurried alongside the driver's window, "Jay, pull up on the curb, as close as you can to the building."

"What?"

"Just fucking do it!"

The uniformed cop backed up and pulled onto the curb, close to the concrete building, just clearing the side view mirror. "Like this?"

Jack didn't answer him. He jumped on the hood and clawed his way to the car's roof. He reached for his gun and pointed up at the window, checking to make sure no one was there. The window was still out of reach by a few feet. He jumped up and crashed back down onto the roof, and a thud sounding much like a shotgun blast echoed inside. He tried once more and this time latched on to the windowpane. He held on, pulling himself up, using all his strength to carry his body to the inside. He lifted his left leg, brought it over the ledge and clung on.

"Jack what the hell do you think you're doing?" Rebecca shouted. "Get down before you kill yourself."

"I'm almost in," he huffed out. With one big push off, he threw himself inside.

"Jack, are you okay?"

No answer.

"Jack?" She looked up, waiting to see if his head would pop up, hoping to see a smile on his face while he tried to catch his breath, but there was none. He didn't cry in pain or laugh in success. He didn't do anything at all.

"Get that backup here now!" she ordered to the uniform, and he repeated her message over the radio.

"Jaaaaacccckk!" she cried out.

* * *

Kennedy sat in the living room and looked around as if she was seeing this place for the first time since she had moved in. Her aunt, the one that Jack had contacted, never showed or called to say she was nearing Massachusetts. There'd been no contact whatsoever from her. That was the least on Kennedy's mind. Kyle was gone, Jack and Rebecca had left. She was home alone in a stranger's house, and she was worried, worried about all of them, about Kyle the most. She didn't know what she would do if anything were to happen to him. The worst thing about this whole ordeal was not knowing if he was alive or dead, or hurt somewhere. Maybe they were arresting people right now and Kyle was safe in the back of a police cruiser while the men with guns did their job. Kyle had done a damn good job of incorporating heart-warm textures in her memories, and that was the sole reason she was not on the floor, bawling, screaming a symphony of sorrow and worry.

She heard footsteps.

Alarm bells went off in her head.

"I won't hurt you!"

The singsongy voice should have been enough to send her running for the front door, screaming for help from nearby neighbors as she ran to the street. She walked out of the living room, through the foyer, and into the hall. It was a phantom voice; perhaps her mind was playing a cruel joke on her. She was also thinking she should call Jack's cell phone number that he had written down for her in case of an emergency, or dial 911. This would be the perfect time.

She blinked and the walls dripped with blood. She stepped back, turned the other way, and it was gone. It was a trick of her mind. Her heart was racing faster than a horse, her chest was tightening, trying to loosen up enough to get air.

"I won't hurt you!" that same melodic voice said again.

She turned in every direction. It was a ghost's voice.

The bathroom door was closed and so was the closet. Plus, the voice didn't sound muffled, it sounded as if it were right over her shoulder. The voice did not sound friendly; it sounded like a lie, like a child promising to his mother that he didn't eat all those Oreos while the evidence of black crumbs was left on his face and teeth.

"Who's there?" she shrieked. She turned left, then right, backing up into the foyer.

Someone was here.

Kennedy spun around the room. "Where are you!?!"

She felt a hard object strike her head. She collapsed to the floor feeling a warm sensation flow around her skull. She felt tired, then she closed her eyes in a deep sleep.

* * *

Jack looked outside and couldn't believe that he was staring at nothing by snow. Rebecca was gone; the car had vanished. And he knew backup would be a lot farther away than he had hoped it would be. Everyone…everything else was gone. He stood in horror, not knowing where he was or where he was heading. He wanted to call out Rebecca's name. He couldn't see her, so what was the point of calling for someone if they weren't there. *Or was she? Was it some sort of illusion?* Jack ruminated. Technology could do wonders nowadays, curing all sorts of diseases, making televisions thinner than pizza boxes, but they still didn't have *Star Trek* technology, or if they did the government hasn't released any such breakthrough.

Jack found himself in a bedroom. It was freshly clean by the look of it—but oh God, was it freezing. It felt like an icebox in there; each of the four winds was blowing, making his leather trench dance in the air and then fall back down.

Jack walked with a purpose. It was an I-don't-give-a-fuck-who's-here walk, a walk that symbolized business: *Hey—I'm a cop and get the fuck out of my way.*

His drew his gun from its holster, gripping it tightly as he hugged the wall. He took a quick peek to the left and saw a dead end. He surveyed the area, listening for the slightest sound of another person.

The smell was overpowering. It was a scent that he was familiar with. Death. It was a terrible nauseating stench that no one could ever really imagine. And it didn't smell like one dead soul, but hundreds. The only thing that stopped Jack from throwing up his guts on the floor was that Kyle was still out there.

Jack went room to room to room, checking each and every opening for Kyle—or anyone else for that matter. He checked close to two dozen rooms but there was no sign of life anywhere. At the end of the long and narrow hallway was an opening that led to a tight-fitted spiral staircase. It was the only way to go. The bottom glowed like an ominous cave with just a speck of light cutting through the granite. Jack concentrated everything he had on the bottom of the spiral metal stairs, praying nothing would pop out and surprise him. He was mostly looking for that fucking weasel Miller. Jack's gut was almost never wrong, and his gut was getting in a whirlwind about this guy.

He walked down the steps softly and lightly, pointing his weapon downward, aiming it at the door. He circled down the stairs at least three times before coming to the end. The room just beyond was long and narrow, filled with water tanks on either side of the room, with some sort of exotic ocean life to the likes that Jack had never seen before. That wasn't a surprise; unless it was a goldfish or some breed of shark, Jack wouldn't have been able to determine what was what anyway.

He walked in the room, surveying the layout. It was a long stretch with a large circular open tank in the middle. He stared at the blue-green water, almost like it was hypnotizing him. There was something soothing and relaxing about being in a place so surreal as this giant aquarium that would most likely rival any aquarium in Boston or San Diego. He felt curiously reassured that Kyle would be fine, but at the same time his mounting fear grew larger.

It was all he could do not to be illogical and start yelling out Kyle's name, hoping that the echo would follow farther than his voice could carry. But he was a rational person after all; he had to do things the right way, the safest way possible, or it could cost him his life—or Kyle's.

He stuck his body close to the left wall, both hands on his gun, gripping it tightly as he edged his way closer. To the right, he noticed the tank's water was darker than it should have been. Then he recognized that familiar gore spread across the steel slats. With no consequence in mind he rushed to the tank, threw his gun back in its holster and lifted himself above the circular opening. He saw a young woman's severed head and he fell backwards. Her eyes were still staring, focused on the ceiling, which had no more details to it than the floor.

*Thank God it's not Kyle.*

He ran to the end of the aquatic room, then stopped dead in his tracks so fast that he almost lost his balance. "My God…" he said as he saw the wallpaper hangings of naked human beings. The stench was unbearable. It smelled like bile and urine and death mixed in some sort of sadistic cocktail. He searched every person's face, looking for a familiar one. There were hundreds lined up along and across the wall; men and woman of all different ages, all different ethnicities. He couldn't tell if Kyle was one of them or not, especially with the bodies that were too far up. He couldn't make them out clearly through the blood and grime that coated their faces. The noises that some of them made gave Jack the familiarity of a neighborhood cat in heat; the shrieking, the groaning.

Standing before him was a death like he had never seen, an imagery that he couldn't imagine being in any slasher or torture-porn film. He was standing before countless bodies, both dead and dying.

This started the last hours of Jack Stoughton's life.

# XVIII

January 30th, 2009 1:18A.M.

Something took over his body. He wasn't quite sure what, but it felt like some kind of high. He felt stronger and tougher, not afraid anymore. He no longer stuck to the shadows, or held out the gun while his bottom lip and hands quivered.

Kyle was doing this for Kennedy now, to save her from whatever might come after her. Until he had the facts down packed it wasn't hard to assume that the same killer (*or killers*) would come after her, too. And from what Chelsea told him, they just might. So stopping the sadistic motherfucker from running the show might just be worth the price of his life.

He found himself in some sort of lounge, like this was an office building (from Hell). There were guys there working, in uniforms and wearing gun belts and masks. What kind of job requires a dress code like that? They looked more like felons robbing a convenience store at two in the morning.

Now his hands were tainted. Blood covered most of his body now. He was a killer. There was no simpler way to say it. He rushed through one of the rooms, emptying an entire clip into four masked men and beating a fifth one into an unconscious state just before he twisted the guy's neck around. Listening to the bones crack, hearing the rattle in the guy's throat, aroused Kyle in a way he never knew possible. Kyle now thought he was crazy, just like one of them. Killing was fun. Killing was fucking awesome! That's what went through his mind shortly afterward. All of his subconscious thoughts attacked him, but only one memory outweighed all of them: Kennedy.

Every room Kyle visited was surrounded by water. And for a brief moment he thought he could have been in an underwater facility, but that couldn't be possible, could it? He was surprised that, with the temperature, the water didn't freeze over. It had to be well below fifty degrees. Everyone, including his victims, wore heavy coats. He had acquired one for himself from a dead body. He'd also stripped each of them of anything that could be used to further his escape. He wondered if escaping Alcatraz back in the day was this brutal, and even if it was, he knew that if you were caught they wouldn't stake your naked ass to the wall on display like some hunted deer.

"That wasn't so bad now, was it?" a static-filled voice echoed from a hidden speaker on some type of PA system.

Kyle looked around, growing angry. His jaw was clenched, his muscles taut and tired. "Who the fuck are you?" he yelled, tears of anger welling in his eyes.

"I am the person you are seeking, I believe," the voice said. "You may call me Mister Miller."

Each hall looked like the last one; each room looked identical to the next. Kyle was stuck in a bombardment of mazes; a maze where entering the wrong room could be the deadliest of mistakes. It was a decision-making situation where even the backup plans needed backup plans.

Kyle had changed this week. He had changed into something that he wanted to kill. Not to say that he'd eat the barrel of a gun, but if or *when* he got free, who he had become would be murdered with what he left behind. He would never let Kennedy see him like this, so frantic, someone who was so capable of taking life. It would be another chapter that he knew she couldn't take—and when he did finally get to her, reach out for her safe, comforting body, he would never mention a word about this. He would never tell her that someone he had hoped to rescue was murdered by what he could only describe as a sea monster, that he had seen hundred of naked men, women, and children staked to walls in some grotesque version of a medieval painting. That was too much for *him* to handle, and he was smack-dab in the middle of the biggest shitstorm he'd ever face.

Survival is everything.

*  *  *  *  *

Jack felt sick after seeing what death looked like.

Its cruel face was now imprinted in his mind forever. He'd smelled the urine and feces that ran down the walls, saw the dead, and saw the dying drawing their last breath. Right now, he wished to God that he had the S.W.A.T. team watching his back. This was one of his few cases where unpredictability was a certainty and getting your ass dead was more likely to happen than not.

He thought of all the things he could have done, things he should have done, like spending more time with his mother, visiting old college friends for a weekend somewhere. Doing things that he had wished he could do, but always found himself too wrapped up in his own work to pursue any kind of a life beyond the badge. The only way he could spend any time with Rebecca was because she *understood*. If it wasn't one investigation, it was another, and if he had vacation time, he would take that time to read his cop novels, in his home, by himself.

The truth was, it hadn't been mere work-related considerations that kept him away from living his life. His rationalization was a legitimate one as far as that went, and it gave him comfort in thinking those were the only reasons he had strayed far away from his friends and family. Maybe there was no real reason. It might have been just an illusion to keep himself convinced that being so far up to the neck with dead bodies and perps to cuff was something he didn't want to bring to his friends and family. His job wasn't the kind you'd sit around the dinner table on Sunday with your loved ones to share the weekly bulletin. Another murder. Another suicide. To Jack, this world was fucked, and it was falling apart so hard and fast that he wasn't sure if the pieces would ever fit back together again. He was a cop. That was his job. He was not, however, some member of a special task force to police the world — maybe that's what was needed out there. World Police — but then who would control *them*? More arrogant bureaucrats looking for their name in the headlines, showing that they were worth the money the taxpayers paid them. They weren't worth shit. They would never change the country, only try to get rich off it so they could retire to a hefty little home somewhere on the beach.

The lights went out.

And flickered back on.

They surrounded him on every side. Men and women, naked, genitals and breasts cut off, blood draining from their bodies, creating a crimson ocean beneath their bare feet.

They weren't human. They couldn't be to survive such injuries and not have the slightest ill affect. They weren't zombies, either; they didn't go after his flesh, they didn't groan with hunger pains for the sweet gooey flesh, that salty skin with a hardy splurge of type O-negative to drink it down with. But they stood in his way — and how did they appear so quickly? The lights couldn't have been out for more than five seconds and now they were just a few yards from him, looking, staring.

Jack didn't want to make any sudden movements. Without knowing what they wanted, he didn't want to give them cause to attack him. There had to be at least a dozen, maybe more. Their facial features gave their genders away, but in every other way they were sexless. They were creatures with a blank stare; it was the kind of stare you got from a vicious dog just moments before it attacked. He felt the same sensation that he got when he was about to serve a warrant on a suspect, that same twitchy-nerve feeling, that flush of heat and cold sweat.

He raised his gun. Fired an array of rounds, most hitting their marks. Only four of the makeshift sexless people fell to the ground, dead — or *deadish.*

He ran. They followed.

Jack shot over his shoulder, panic fire.

He followed a long corridor down to the depths of the unknown. They still followed. He fired over his shoulder until the gun clicked empty.

The walls were a rusted brown of metal and bolts. He ran for another fifty yards before entering another room and closing the door securely behind him, locking them out.

They pounded on the door; loud, violent thuds.

Jack slid to the ground trying to catch his breath. It was only the beginning.

Detective Jack Stoughton of the Snow Hill Police Department had another obstacle at hand. It was neither human nor beast, or not a beast that he was ever familiar with.

It stood before him large and scaly, at least a hundred feet long with a jaw that could crush automobiles effortlessly. Its eyes were cat-like, and they were scanning him. He wasn't locked inside anymore. Jack had managed to find himself a way out into some sort of backwoods.

Snow covered the trees as if in a wonderland dream, and it would have been a beautiful dream had it not been for the monster that looked back at Jack as if he had pissed it off somehow.

It growled some strange thunder.

Jack slowly lifted himself up off the cold ground, brushed his jacket off, and holstered his gun.

"Listen big guy, I don't mean harm," Jack tried to reason with it.

In a loud, echoing voice, it replied, "This is our home."

Jack was dumbfounded to find that it could speak, speak clearly, speak his language. "I don't mean to disturb you. I'm just looking for a way out."

"Death is the only way out," it growled.

Its snout was that of a dragon, its claws like a wild cheetah. It looked part reptilian, whatever it was. It was green with long, black stripes racing down the side, and just a pinch of red blotches on its foot-long toes. Jack didn't want to believe that God could concoct an abnormality of such great proportions.

Jack hugged the building, still listening to the tireless effort of bangs and knocks on the steel door. He sidestepped his way along the building, looking for a clear-cut path to anywhere but here.

The door broke loose.

*Sometimes you just can't win.* The thought occurred to him. It was like ordering fast food for $5.42 and realizing that you only had a five dollar bill in your wallet. *It's the little fucking things that annoy us the most. And when things don't go right, oh, they fucking don't go right at all.*

The monster growled at the sexless people, still with blood draining out of them and now looking like blood-red body paint. They staggered like drunks on a Saturday night just after last call. Now they were acting more like a George Romero flick. The beast, as if defending its young, swiped at them, taking two of them out. With its long, sharp claws he easily sliced them into several pieces, their insides sprawled on the snow that had now turned a dark red. The snow mound gave way to the warmth of their blood which now looked coagulated. In most cases this occurs several hours after death, not just a few minutes, but Jack wasn't going to walk over and give it a good look; his concentration was on getting the fuck away from the monster and those fucking mindless souls.

He ran fast and hard, his breath forming in front of his face. He was gaining speed and putting that evil place far behind him. Most of the mindless souls were dead, thanks to that reptilian beast. It had sliced them up real good, better than any grocery store deli could slice meat.

Jack leaned against a large tree trunk, and in the balance of midnight moon, he gathered himself as he would any other case, assessing the situation before determining a course of action. But then he threw caution to the wind and winged it.

He loaded his gun with a second clip.

Jack thought, *time for round two you fuckers.*

\* \* \*

*Think I'll have me a nice jerk*, Miller thought. This kind of bad ass mumbo-jumbo turned him on, aroused him in a way that he thought a woman could never do. So he sat behind the desk, unzipped his pants, took out his erected penis, and began doing his activity for the night. In his mind, imagery was the real key to the success; it would make him blow his load a lot quicker. He thought of the killings, the deaths, the midnight monsters. The things people were too chicken shit to admit existed. He knew about them. He knew secrets that most people would give their left nut for, and that's what got him off.

After a few minutes, he released his load onto the floor, creating another matching streak stain. Then he leaned back in his leather chair and relaxed. He had nothing to worry about. Everything was on schedule. That's what had gotten him excited again. He knew what was coming next. My God, did he fucking love it.

There were no more pressing matters to deal with. The girl was dead and the children had all been sacrificed to Him. The day was nearly upon them: February second. He saw no significance to this date. It was a Monday, but that was really no importance at all save for the working sap's nine-to-five. He never told Miller much more than he needed to know to get the job done. Maybe it was foolish to believe in everything he had been told that night over thirty years ago. It still stuck in his mind, as fresh as the day it happened.

*The moonlight shone through the windows peacefully, melting onto the hardwood floors in George's room. The snow had finally stopped. The news said that it was the worst storm to hit this side of the world in a decade. But it was over now. The blizzard had subsided and retreated back into its cold upbringings.*

*George lay awake in bed. He was home on vacation from Snow Hill Community College. He had had enough of school anyway. If his parents didn't force him to go, he would have just stayed home, reading his books that he cherished so much, watching midday talk shows, and probably ending up being a fat lazy cliché working at a fast food joint and earning a intolerable income.*

*George had just turned nineteen a few weeks before, and though he had a few friends and family that lived nearby show up, he felt alone and awkward, as if he was embarrassed to gain a year. A couple more and he could officially go on his first drinking binge.*

*He stirred underneath the flannel sheets. Nothing much was on his mind that should keep him from falling asleep at one in the morning. He rose out of bed, went to his window, and stared out. There were snowmen lined up at every house. Not just the occasional one or two on the block that kids would build with their parents but dozens and dozens. They moved. They glided across the unsoiled blanket of snow toward his house. Like all snowmen, they bore no emotions but a carved smile. But something about them was just evil. They were closing in at a steady pace. George told himself they couldn't get in the* house, though — they'd melt into puddles, and it'd be the old story of *Frosty the Snowman* all over again.

In a waking nightmare, he realized that they were coming for him. He wasn't sure how he knew, but he just did. Was that even possible? Could snowmen come to life and snag you in the middle of the night? No. It would be lunacy to think that.

The snowmen formed a straight line in front of his window like marching soldiers, silently beckoning George to come out into the cold and brutal weather. He stood there for several minutes, just looking in horror at the sight of the living snowmen.

The awful dreams that had been recurring every night for the past couple of weeks came back to him, and like this there was a certain surreal flavor to them. He knew from the moment he stepped onto the hardwood of his bedroom, feeling the cold floor, that this was no dream. He was awake, alert and, to some extent, nervous. Truth be told, he was scared shitless.

He thought of waking his parents up to have them witness this odd imagery of snowmen lining up to get a look-see at good ole Georgey boy staring out of his second floor bedroom window. The snowmen neither looked up nor paid any attention to him — but George Miller paid a whole lot of attention to them. And that's what they wanted.

Every night for a week they had shown up at his window, as if to say hello, though they said nothing at all. They would just stand there, and by morning they would be gone.

One night when it wasn't as cold as the other nights had been, George stepped outside and waited for them. Sure enough, just past midnight, they lined up again. He was standing there, looking at the snowmen and wondering how on Earth this was even possible. Maybe he was delusional. Just some kid who was seeing snowmen walk — not walk — glide to his house every night to keep him company. That would be a good reason to make a month's worth of appointments with the best psychiatrist insurance would cover. If he did tell anyone, nobody would ever believe him. And he wouldn't. He liked having this secret to himself. It gave him some sense of purpose, something to look forward *to, and in Snow Hill, he had three long months to do this every night if he so choose to.*

*In less than fifty feet, George had walked from his comfortably warm bedroom into the bitter cold yard. And on the day he did that, March eighteenth to be exact, the snowmen did something to him. Most people would have called it an implant (those would be the UFO nuts), but he called it an injection of truth. Suddenly things that were hazy became clear. Information about a world long forgotten rose from the depths of its burial from centuries ago, and now the world didn't seem like a world anymore. It felt like lies – all of it. Just little white lies that faith and belief covered up so well, so that no one could see the light of day anymore. No one knew the truth, except for maybe God, but wasn't he part of it, too? George didn't know. That was one thing that was left unanswered to him.*

*Through the field of snowmen one figure stood out among the crowd. A scrawny, ice-blue-faced man that didn't quite seem like a man at all. George felt a chill race down his spine, and he wasn't sure if it was the cold temperature or the sight of the man in a long wool coat and top hat looking as though he belonged in a very strange 1940s movie.*

*From that moment forth, George Miller had been serving Him and carrying out His deeds until the time was right, in anticipation for the new beginning.*

Now George had everything in place; everything was lined up in accordance to the way *He* wanted them to be. The children's souls had been taken, their innocent blood drained into a large fountain so that He could bathe in it. It was on the rise, the new world, the new Snow Hill. And for everyone else Miller would say, "Fuck 'em. It's my destiny, not theirs."

\* \* \*

The room was filled with blood.

Kyle wished he'd never found it. But one room led to another that led to another. And now, before him stood a fountain, the biggest one he'd ever seen, filled with thick red liquid. It gave off a certain odor; when blood mixes with certain organs the smell is unique to quite possibly anything else. There were torches along the side, lit with dancing flames, which gave the room more of a Satanic feel. But Kyle never once thought that devil worshipping was to blame here, just a bunch of sick fucked-up people with too much time on their hands.

He stood against one of the concrete walls and stared at the large flowing fountain. Another room waited on the other side of the crescent-shaped blood bath. It had no unusual markings or designs. It was plain and bland, matching the rest of the facility.

Finally, Kyle walked to the other room, feeling bile build up in the back of his throat, but controlling it enough not to puke all over himself. This next room wasn't much larger than Kyle. It was bare, filled with shadows and no light. A steel door waited across from him, battered and bruised. He opened it and a cold chill snuck its way into the already frostbitten air.

He had found the way outside. He had escaped — or had he?

There was nothing but snow and backwoods, and a moon streaming down. And a man. A man with a large overcoat and hat and a walking stick. He was skinny and frail. His face was drained of color, like a body at the morgue. He walked over to Kyle, slowly, nonthreateningly, and stared at him with his bony exterior.

"There are more tasks ahead of you," he said in a kind elderly voice.

Something about this man didn't seem right. He seemed like a ghost, like a phantom making a rare appearance, and through the cold air and the snow, Kyle saw something beyond the trees, beyond everything he could see. It glowed a brilliant bright light, echoing toward the heavens.

"Who are you?" Kyle asked through shivering lips.

"I am who shall not be named," he replied, then walked away in a patient stride.

"Wait!" Kyle yelled. "Stop. Come baaaacck."

But the man was too far gone to hear him over the howling wind, and even if he did hear, he might not have turned back. Kyle didn't chase after him.

Kyle realized, for a brief second, what that man really looked like—frozen death. His eyes were black, darker than any abyss and colder than the climate of space.

It began to snow again. Kyle looked up past the tree branches to the darkened sky and wondered where he was going, what he was doing.

His hands were shaking; the cold air made it hard to breathe, but he forced himself to continue on.

# XIX

January 30th, 2009 1:49A.M.

Kennedy dreamed something awful.

*He appeared to her in a shimmering white glow. A person dressed in a white robe. She followed him.*

*It was morning; a clear, blue sky with the sun hanging warmly. Trees and plants grew all around her in some sort of out-of-this-world vista of glorious days. It was beautiful. It was a heaven. The landscape seduced her, the fresh air tickled at her skin, and the field of green looked like emeralds. It was the purest green grass she had ever seen in her life as she walked barefoot and felt the ground beneath her toes.*

*But in the daybreak, the sky turned to an overcast of grey, unsettling clouds, and in the center of the sky directly above her, like a plasma fire, the sky shot out into a brilliant white, with radiant flames forcing their way around her, engulfing her and lifting her back to the sky.*

*She was gone.*

*Kennedy found herself in a wasteland, calling out Kyle's name, but the only response was her own voice echoing back to her, proving once again how alone she really was, how scared and terrified she really felt.*

*She saw the dead and the dying nailed to walls, body parts scattered the floor; severed hands and feet lie amidst the pile, and the blood was seeping through their rotting skin as it peeled back in its decaying form. She covered her mouth and clenched her nose to hold off the stench a little bit longer. She walked the halls of Death's mansion, found an old cupboard, and pulled out a piece of paper that looked like it had been rubbed in dirt. It had writings on it; none that she could understand. They looked like a cross between ancient hieroglyphics and a young child's scribbles. She put it back inside. It was the only item in the cupboard. She stared at the rotted wooden cupboard trying to make sense of that chicken scratch she had just seen.*

*Kennedy recalled with great clarity the last time she had seen drawings quite as unique as that. It was her ninth grade project on Egypt and the pyramids and the people and the culture. Similar markings were scrawled out through hundreds of rooms in pyramids, all proclaiming the greatest love and joy or damning them straight to the underworld.*

*A man with a pale blue face walked up next to her, grabbing her shoulder.*

*She screamed.*

Kennedy woke up tied and gagged on the floor of a garage or basement. She couldn't quite tell where she was. It had that strong odor of age and mildew; boxes were stacked on top of boxes that were covered by a blue tarp. Small rectangular windows lined the side.

It must be a garage.

She could smell the faint scent of gasoline.

No one else was with her.

She struggled to sit up, but her hands were bound behind her back and her legs were tied at the knees and ankles. A single strip of duct tape concealed her mouth and stopped her from yelling out for help, which to her meant someone could hear her if she made a lot of noise. It could cause suspicion and a noisy neighbor might just come along and stumble upon her, call the police, and then she'd be free.

Rebecca and Jack wouldn't even know she was missing, not until they returned, unless they phoned her. Though they might not get too worried until the fourth or fifth call went unanswered.

If only she could find out where the hell she was.

She searched around, rocking back and forth to get a panoramic view of everything. There were tools hung on the walls by nails and screws. An old beat-to-hell radio sat on a scuffed-up workstation. Odd parts for motors lined another section of the garage. This person was a mechanic or knew a lot about cars. She could tell a lot from a person's personal area. She called it a "gift." Somehow, from the way someone assembled their bedroom or bathroom or garage, it was easy for Kennedy to tell who a person was. Kyle had joked with her a hundred times about being a profiler for the police or FBI. She always thought he was kidding, but she had the potential to be a damn good profiler.

"Please don't be afraid," a man's voice called out.

She looked around the room but couldn't find the owner of the voice.

"I'm sorry I had to take such measures, but I needed to make sure it was still you."

He stepped into her sight. His brown leather boots were the first things she could see, then his blue jeans, his white t-shirt and bleak leather jacket. His face was taut and strained. His expression was sincere and stern.

"I will not hurt you. I promise," he assured her. "I'm going to cut you lose. Please don't run or scream, okay?"

Kennedy shook her head in compliance.

"My name is Daniel," he told her as he pulled a pocket knife out of his back pocket. "They guy who clobbered you is dead." He cut the tape from her ankles, then her knees. "I made it there just in time, but I must say I was trying to find—I guess he'd be your boyfriend, Kyle." He removed the tape from her wrists, and last her mouth.

"Why do you want Kyle?" was the only thing she could think of to ask. Not why he had tied her up or why he had taken her—or killed who?

"He's special to the survival." He looked away from her, almost ashamed. "I know you'll think I'm some lunatic if you don't already, so I won't bore you with details. I need to find Kyle before it's too late."

"Before what's too late?"

"Where is he?" he snapped.

"We don't know," she confessed. "They went looking for him."

"They?"

"Jack and Rebecca. They're cops."

"*Sonofabitch!*"

His angry words frightened her, but what scared her more was that he knew Kyle, or knew *of* Kyle. And now he was talking about survival. My God, what a whack job! He was probably some perverted man just fresh out of prison looking for young girls to screw. She closed her mind to the thought, and picked herself up off the ground. Daniel gestured to help her up, but she refused. She backed herself up to the scuffed up work station in the back of the garage.

"What do you what with me?" she asked through trembling lips.

"Nothing. I saved you," he told her. "Please do not be afraid of me. I'm here to help."

*You just had me tied up and I'm supposed to trust you?*

He stared into her eyes as if he had read her thoughts, but he couldn't. He wasn't psychic or possessed with any supernatural powers; none that Kennedy was aware of anyway.

The man resembled an urban cowboy. He was attractive in an action-movie-superstar sort of way. He was built, and the jeans around his calves showed this off. He walked to the front of the garage and peeked out the window. The moonlight was casting shadows.

"I've been tracking something that's almost as old as Earth itself," he said calmly. "Now, before you go thinking I'm some crackerjack nutcase that belongs in a padded room, my family died some years ago. My mother and father and two brothers."

"I'm sorry..."

He turned to look at her, gave a sympathetic nod. "It was because something was going on that I couldn't quite understand, then I started looking into it. First my younger brother went missing, then my other brother. It was too much of a coincidence that both my brothers turned up missing within a few months. Police found no clues or bodies so they assumed it was just a runaway case. I never believed it for a minute."

"What happened?" she asked curiously.

"They were bartered, I guess you could say." He turned to look back out the window, scanning the street. "My parents were promised some kind of glorious heaven if they were to give up their children. And you know there are more parents in this world that would do that than not, it's all over the fucking news nowadays; parents leaving their kids at the mall; parents abusing and killing their children; mothers and father neglecting their infant children, leaving them in cars or at the park while they go do whatever it is that's so important for them to do. And because of their gross stupidity, their children die from sun exposure, or are kidnapped, raped and murdered by some wanted pedophile running loose. It's everywhere you look. I just never believed my parents would ever be the kind to do such a thing. Maybe your parents seemed like the greatest in the world..."

"They hated me," she admitted. "I don't think there was one thing they liked about me, especially my drunken father."

"I'm sorry."

She gave the same thank you nod as he had given her. "But what do you mean they bartered your brothers? I mean, what's going on? And why are you looking for Kyle?"

"I like to read," he said. "Can't get enough of it. When I did some reading to try and solve whatever the hell was going on, I found something in a book that had no name, no author. It was in a leather-bound case; the pages were old and stained with time. I found it on eBay from someone I tried to track down, but as soon as the book was sold, the account was cancelled and I never did find out who that person was.

The book told about certain areas in the world—all over the world, actually—where there are what they call mouths. They open up to another place. You're still here on Earth, but in another dimension, so to speak. There are technical terms for everything, but unless you've done the reading or research I've done, you wouldn't know what the hell I was talking about."

"I still don't understand."

"You want something to drink?" he offered.

She was a bit thirsty. "Sure."

"Let's go in the house."

# XX

January 30th, 2009 2:14A.M.

Daniel explained everything as best he could.

Kennedy sat there in his kitchen staring out the window above the sink. She was taking deep breaths, trying to let all this information settle into her brain, but it just seemed too fictional to believe; it just didn't make sense, everything he was saying just couldn't make sense.

Mouths to other dimensions. Hell. Supernatural beings. These were all part of his explanation. But what kind of explanation was that? It sounded like a tale of fiction, or an institutionalized man's ramblings. Maybe both. This man who had bound her legs and hands could be one hell of a nut, maybe escaped from some psych hospital, maybe a convict out on parole, as so many criminals these days are.

"I know this is hard to take in," he said, then sipped his coffee. "A long time ago, almost before time itself, there was something written—a book. It was allegedly written by a demon, one who possessed the secret to travel dimensionally, through worlds, through space; maybe through time for all I know. Fuck, I don't know. I just know the signs have led me to this place."

"What kind of signs?"

"Dreams. Visions."

She shuffled her feet nervously under the kitchen chair. "What about Kyle?" she asked.

"Kyle was just a kid in a dream," Daniel told her with finality. "He's already crossed over to somewhere else, to the next world. I just don't know where it is. It's like traveling the ocean where there are still uncharted islands; each world is like an uncharted island, it's tough to say what kind of world it is going to be. Anything *or* everything could be different. And

203

maybe it's not even another world but Hell itself." He got up from the chair that sat across from Kennedy, walked on the scuffed tile floor to the kitchen sink, placed his empty mug in it, and ran the water. "It's like the Holy Bible. People with strong enough beliefs would give their life for such a book, but there have been different versions, variations throughout the years. With this book, <u>Necromancer,</u> as they call it, there are supposedly six volumes that were made thousands of years ago. And each variation is supposed to reveal the secret to open the gates to the Underworld, the Afterlife, Hell—whatever name you prefer. When you match up these variants, you can find a path that will lead you to any opening to Hell. It's like a spell book." He tried it simplify it for her, "You cast a spell, so to speak."

"This can't be real," she said.

"But it is."

"Why aren't people doing something to stop this then?"

"Who's going to fight off demons?" he laughed. "You think the FBI has a special task force for something like this? Their minds are so closed off. All they can see are homeland attacks, but no one ever thinks about global attacks, another type of life with so much strength and knowledge that the world could be crippled in a matter of hours."

Kennedy stood up and backed herself against the white paneled wall. Somehow all this information just wasn't sinking in. It was too surreal, too impossible to take in in just an hour; it needed careful consideration. From her understanding this was the end of the world, and Kyle, Jack, Rebecca and every other poor son of a bitch on Earth was stuck in the middle of a war they knew nothing about.

"I need to stop it," Daniel told her. "Only people like me can."

"People like you?"

"People with knowledge of the events at hand. People all over the world are tracking these holes down to stop them. Some will die a most agonizing death, and some will come out the victor. I hope it's the latter for me."

She nodded, hoping it was the case, too. If what he was saying was true, then he was her only hope, and Kyle's only hope. *My God, where the hell is Kyle?*

Kennedy was exhausted; her head still throbbed in a spiraling pain caused by whoever had knocked her silly. That was another thing Daniel hadn't mentioned. Who had done it? It could have been him for all she knew. It's not like she'd seen the bastard who did it. She was too scared to look, but half-hoped she'd get a glimpse of her assailant before the final blow that had rendered her unconscious.

"Daniel," she said nervously, "who hit me?"

"I don't know." He shook his head. "By the time I came in, you were on the ground and a man with a ski mask was hovering over you. I thought he was going to kill you. I chased him off," he explained, "but then I came back to make sure you were okay. I tossed you in the back of my truck, brought you here, and taped you up just in case you had *changed*."

"Changed?"

"Demons take on all forms."

"Right. Demons."

"I know you don't believe me. You don't have to." He smiled halfheartedly. "Not too many people do. If you mentioned what I told you three hundred years ago, you'd be set on fire at the stake; they believed back then."

"This isn't three hundred years ago," she said.

"No. But if you believe in God, you must believe in Satan and Evil. It's like the sun and the moon; two opposites that come together with day and night."

"I'm sorry," Kennedy said anxiously. "I just don't believe in this bullshit."

"I know. No need to be sorry."

He gestured for her to follow him. She did. To the living room. The carpet was commercial grey and the walls a kind of taupe. "Why don't you rest for a little bit," he offered. "I promise I won't tie you up this time."

She gave an awkward smile, and took him up on his offer. She sat on the solid blue couch and rested her head on the soft matching pillow. Her eyes closed, and she drifted off into a long-awaited sleep.

Daniel went upstairs to his bedroom. He locked the door behind him, walked over, and closed the blinds.

Out in the wee hours of the morning, the cold winter night called.

Daniel lay on his bed, flat on his back. He positioned the pillow comfortably under his head, closed his eyes peacefully, and willed himself into his dreams again, a power that he had learned to master. It allowed him to travel to any point of his memory, even his vague memories at birth, of coming out of the womb for the very first time, of the first breath he ever took. But now was not the time to reminisce over past memories but to look to the future, using his ability to see things through remote viewing.

He could see Kyle.

*Kyle walked toward the bright light coming from the ground.*

*It was alive. The mouth was just that: a mouth, with sharp teeth and skin; it was a manhole made of flesh, of real skin from something otherworldly. But the bright light still promised a sense of comfort and a dreary calling. Like the night outside, it called to Kyle. Come closer, boy.*

*Just a bit closer!*

*Kyle listened intently, and he followed the voice through the backwoods until the light was so overpowering it gave him a glow of extraordinary power, as if he were a higher being.*

*It swallowed him whole.*

*It left him in a spiral of overwhelming fear, something that he couldn't control or release himself from; he was a prisoner by his own mind. Whatever powered the white light took control over Kyle, consumed him – and gave him answers to questions he did not even know to ask.*

A sickening image entered Daniel's dream and cast the other one aside:

*Men and women spiked and stuck on poles. Blood smeared over their naked bodies. Some were mothers in the midst of giving birth, the umbilical cords stretched out from between their limp legs. The newborns were gone.*

*The men had lost their penises to the thrall of a sharp object. They were still bleeding, and either dead or about to be. The steel walls from which they hung was corroded in a crimson river; streams of blood raced down the walls and created a puddle of death. Hundreds of dead men and woman filled the wall up like slots at a casino, side-by-side, above and below. There was no escaping it. Death had found its victims here.*

Daniel cried. Through his cold tears of pain he let out a sob that was neither loud nor hostile. He slept, unaware of his ambiguous actions. To him, he was trying to find Kyle, and find a way to stop what could potentially be the worst thing the world had ever seen.

Daniel had traveled to Italy, Mexico, Africa, and Egypt, all to find some clue, some hard evidence that would support his claims if he ever needed to take it to the government. But then who was he? A simple salesman who had stumbled upon something in a barn on the outskirts of Ohio a decade ago and had now appointed himself—as many others had—to be mankind's savior. He sold tractors for a living and barely made enough to sleep at sleazy hotels and order a burger when he got really hungry. He was just a man who read a lot, books that seemed too real for them to be labeled as fiction, but that's how fiction starts off, isn't it? With something real, something true to the earth, something you can point at, touch, see, smell. A legend or folklore, a dream or a real life event posted on the evening news. That's how it always starts.

The truth was coming.

*He saw a new man, an older man, in a dark brown trench with a gun and a badge dangling from a metal chain around his neck. He was a cop.*

*His gun was pointed at the ground as he crept from side to side, using all of his police training for hostile environments, only at the academy they teach you to stay on your toes at all times and have backup — not to go to other worlds.*

*Bits of vomit stained the bottom of his coat; red-orange chunks stuck on it like glue. He had seen the same image, the wall of dead people. It might have been more humane to fill up a basement with water and let them all slowly drown. They would beg for their lives, but it wouldn't be like this. Jesus, not like this.*

*The cop wandered disconsolately, eagerly in search of the kid.*

*It came out of nowhere. A thing the size of a giant, with large green hands and yellow eyes, and hair that frayed back like a horse. It was angry, down right pissed off. But fuck — what the hell was it?*

*The cop shot it seven times in the chest and never missed once. But it kept coming.*

*The cop ran, firing over his shoulder, looking for someplace to duck into.*

*It charged after him, and in a single swipe of his long, gnarling claws...*

Daniel woke up in a cold sweat that had soaked his pillow and left a ring around his shirt. He sprung up like a jack-in-the-box, breathing heavily and trying hard to erase the images from his head. But it was futile. They weren't going anywhere at all. They would stay there, stamped in his mind, scarring what was left of his sanity.

*And Kennedy must still be sleeping downstairs*, he thought. He hoped he hadn't woken her. There was no telling what kind of noises or yelling he might make when he was in one of his dreams. At his last apartment a neighbor had called the police because it sounded as though there was a murder happening, and the poor seventy-year-old woman nearly had a heart attack. After that, he promised himself never to live in an apartment building, with the walls so cheap and paper thin; he didn't want to be the cause of someone's grandmother's death.

He remembered the first sign.

Scrawlings all over a broken down gas station off Route 7 just outside of Westchester. There were symbols of the most demonic kind, as if a Satanist was trying to conjure up a dark spirit. It took over three months for him to translate the writings. And then it became clear to him, clear as anything had ever been to Daniel. It read: HELL IS AMONG US AT THE CENTER OF TIME.

The writings didn't make much sense until he heard rumors about a book called Necromancer. It was apparently a book that had been written many centuries ago by Satan's apprentice. His name was Douglas Lanford. It was 1721 A.D. and six volumes of this work were made before Lanford was killed by a blazing fire in the middle of town. The townspeople cheered and chanted hateful slurs to the devil worshiper; they threw stones and sticks, anything to leave a lasting impression, as his flesh melted away into boils and gooey puddles of a person that once was.

There were many fabled stories of the Necromancer volumes, and even fake versions listed on eBay going for thousands of dollars. Just another person's get-rich-quick scheme.

One of the true <u>Necromancer</u> volumes was here in Snow Hill.

The signs and visions pointed to it. To an untitled bounded book that sat on an altar somewhere beneath the city in a catacomb of the dead. And Daniel was not going to let it fall into the wrong hands; he was not going to let the world be overturned by Evil.

He stood up, wiping the sweat from his head with the end of his shirt, staining it with perspiration. He glanced out the window. The sun was on the rise yet he could still see the stars. He made a wish. Soon the stars went away and day began.

Today was a day of reckoning.

Today was a day where Daniel would risk his life and soul to find that book.

Today was a day where he would put one of the pieces of the puzzle right.

Today he would die.

# XXI

January 30th, 2009 6:58A.M.

Jack thanked his lucky stars that the creature didn't kill him.

The throbbing pain echoed around his face where three long, deep gashes creviced his cheek. It would leave a scar. He was lucky. He had shot it four times before it slowed down — not stopped, but slowed down. Then Jack found the nearest exit and ran outside into the bitter cold.

He cornered himself against the building as it began to snow once more. He saw a light off in the distance. It was powerful, like on a landing strip or a lighthouse. He was attracted to it, like a long-lost loved one thought dead but found again. He paid close attention to it and nothing else. It called out to him, told him to come closer, begged him to come near. It wanted him, needed him.

*That's right Jacky-boy! Come closer!*

He walked a straight, steady line to the aurora, passing the field of trees that might have seemed rather beautiful if not for the place they were in.

It sure wasn't Snow Hill anymore.

As Jack got closer, the voice got louder inside his head. *That's right. You're almost here Jacky-boy! Almost here indeed.*

The light shot up from the ground like a cannon of unparalleled fire. It came to him in almost orgasmic waves of undiluted pleasure.

But beyond that he saw a man's face — the face of a devil.

Jack was mere feet away when something emerged from a crack in the soil. It was a man, or at least it seemed like a man.

211

His face and body were not visible due to the brightness of the light that was overshadowing him to such a great extent that all you could see was a hazed glow of a figure.

Kyle swept in and tackled Jack to the ground, slammed his body into the snow. Then he took the stolen gun and fired three rounds at the figure. The man-creature went down in a screeching blaze, like a dying walrus on the shoreline.

Kyle pressed down on Jack's chest, just above his heart, to hold him steady, calm him down as he tried to talk to him.

"Jack, it's Kyle!"

Jack struggled, tossing and turning, finally knocking the limp gun out of Kyle's hand with a blow to the wrist, then twisting him over into a chokehold. Kyle pushed on Jack's stomach repeatedly to get him release him. Kyle was unable to speak; the air was draining from his lungs.

Jack released him.

Kyle rolled off onto his back beside him. "Nice to see you, too, Jack," he gasped.

"What the fuck is going on?"

"I don't even know where to began," he said, trying to catch his breath. "We've got sea serpents, demons, and a lot of dead people."

"I saw," Jack shuttered. He looked at the light now knowing what it really was—a death trap. It called you until it brought you close enough for one of its minions to grab you and hang you on the steel wall like a naked decoration.

Now that Jack had broken away from the hold of the light calling to him, it was pitch black. There wasn't a single star in the sky; no moon hovered above. The only light was from the white snow that clung to everything.

"Where's Kennedy?"

"She's at home," Jack told him, regaining his composure. "Rebecca's waiting in the car, probably scared shitless right now."

*What if she followed me in?* he thought.

Jack jumped to his feet, then helped Kyle up. "Sorry about the..."

"No problem."

Jack saw the gun he had knocked loose. "Get the gun. You'll need it."

Under normal circumstances, he would have taken the gun and holstered it to his waistband, but this was anything but normal. And Kyle had probably just saved his life.

Kyle picked up the gun that now only had three more shells left in it, thinking he'd better make them count for all they were worth.

They headed back to the facility with purpose. They were going to walk out the front door and pretend like none of this had ever happened. Perhaps Jack would call the FBI to have them look into these premises further, but this was way out of his department's league. Plus, he was almost certain that within some branch of the Federal Government there was a splinter group that handled matters of the extreme such as this. Or maybe this was totally out of their control. No, not maybe. *It was.*

Jack suggested that, rather than walking through the building this time, it would be less hazardous to walk *around* it. There was no telling what lurked in any of the other rooms in this great big mansion of horror.

The cold picked up, whipping their faces, thickening the air. It was so dark out it seemed that the stars had long died out in the heavens. They followed the building to the front.

It all looked the same as when they'd left it. They were on the same street, next to the same buildings. Jack looked around, stunned and confused. *Where was everything?*

"What the fuck is going on?" Kyle asked, barely above a whisper.

The streetlights that lined either side were broken. No lights came from any of the buildings or the far off residences. This was the darkened future, an abomination from Hell— actually, this was Hell, or a close replica of it. And Hell had apparently frozen over, as the old saying went.

"Where are we?" Jack looked to Kyle.

"Chelsea mentioned this," he explained vaguely.

"Who?"

"This girl—she's dead."

Jack looked at him, not so much sympathetically that Kyle had seen someone die but dumbfounded as to what the hell was going on. He looked tired and worn. He folded his arms to save any precious heat he could.

"She told me that this is another world," Kyle said. It was an explanation that needed more than just a few words, something along the lines of a series of books to fully explain the complexity of their predicament and how to rectify the situation instead of being stuck in a world where monstrosities were as common as beer commercials.

She had mentioned something to Kyle while they were barricading themselves in the wall. She had told him about a room deep underground. It had the answers, she told him; to escape, to come and go as you please, actually. But Kyle was more hell-bent on escaping than traveling back and forth or— God forbid—going to someplace far worse than this. However, Kyle knew they had to go *in* before they could get *out*.

Kyle looked down at the snow-covered ground, looked back at Jack, and said, "Follow me."

* * *

Daniel left a note for Kennedy before he took off. The streets were sapped down to the hard ice and snow, the stuff plows didn't want to touch because if they dropped the plow too low they'd be taking half the street with them too.

He left in his less-than-stellar Mitsubishi. He liked the car, despite the rusted, multicolored hood and the cracked windshield. It ran well, got him to where he was going, and was good with mileage.

He drove to the Snow Hill Country Club. There wasn't a big giveaway sign that read WEIRD SHIT HAPPENS HERE in big bold letters on a billboard with lights surrounding it and that annoying yet recognizable music like an ice cream truck on a warm summer day staking out local parks for kids with their mommy's dollar bills.

It looked like an average establishment, on an average street, in an average city. It was as tall and as wide and as big as five houses, and the lawn seemed like it would have been beautiful in the springtime. Massachusetts is beautiful in the spring, especially around the Boston Harbor; ships coming in at night, stars coming out, a nice gentle breeze blowing in from the ocean in cool strides on his face. In all honesty, it would have made a lovely greeting card.

The book was all he could think about. It contained messages from the Evil Ones, ways to transport from world to world, to be invincible. Necromancer is, or as legend precedes it, the most evil thing ever conceived in the world. And it belonged to Daniel. It was his. He came all this way for it, and he'd be damned if he would let someone else — a non-believer — get their grips on it.

Since there were police cars surrounding the club—half on the curb, half on the street—he parked around the corner. *They have no idea what they're getting themselves into,* he thought.

Daniel saw the broken window above, surrounded in a perfect rectangle by snow. He stayed clear and went around back, hoping the police had not covered the entire building. He walked down the side then turned into the back alley of the building. It was lit by blue flashing lights strobing off the ground but was abandoned save for a green dumpster sitting alone in one corner.

He found no door but there was something odd about the back wall. He could tell it was out of place, like the cement was not created with the rest of the building. A certain bulge gave away its secrets. Like a blind man trying to walk carefully, he felt his way along, using his sense of touch and blocking out all else. It felt hollow right in the center. Daniel looked up and down and saw a small uprising in the center of the wall, enough to let air through. He pushed on it with all his might, and it moved. It sounded like a cinder block being dragged on asphalt as it pushed back, allowing access to a hidden entrance.

Through the darkness, he went into the room.

The concrete ground sloped downward. The walls were painted with paneled borders, as if it was someone's house. That's what it looked like: the walls were a pale blue, decorated with oak trimming. There were three doors, one on each wall. And it called out to him, called him to make a choice, a choice that could lead him simply into a closet or to his demise. Daniel had no fear; he had nothing to be afraid of. He knew very well what he was up against. And though it might not seem like it with his hesitations, he was prepared, ready to take on whatever came into his path, whatever would try and stop him from getting that book.

For the past years, he'd searched the globe for the unthinkable treasure, for things that only gathered in fairytales and folk legends. He was possessed by intrigue, lured by an element that called out to him—that reached out to him and took him by the hand. Finding ancient texts on walls in Egypt was gratifying, finding The Book of the Dead buried off the coast of Mexico was even more intoxicating, but being able to collect the unspoken volumes of Necromancer would have been that much better; to travel where no man has set foot, to visualize what else was beyond this world.

He looked around, smiled wickedly, and laughed heavily as if life was its own joke. He was crazy; crazy and sinister; crazy and sinister and evil. His intentions were for his own gain, not the betterment of man, which was a rule that had been spoken down throughout the centuries, a rule that should be respected. Rules were overrated anyway, Daniel thought. They were meant to be broken. That's what they were made for: To tempt us, to urge us to bypass them like a highway speed limit sign.

He broke the rules.

*Joseph McGee*

# XXII

January 30th, 2009 8:12A.M.

This was like an evil theme park waiting to eat young, eager children.

The basement showed abnormalities in scratchings and paintings; hybrids, homemade beasts, and one Supreme Being that had a body of a god, large curled horns that looked like a ram, and intent in its eyes. But Kyle saw them as nothing more than engravings and ran his fingers along the wall, outlining each marking in perfect harmony. He stared in awe like a kid on a school trip to the museum, wondering who had done them and why; simple questions, but equally volatile. Jack went ahead down the lone walkway of an underground tomb that reminded him of those *Indiana Jones* movies. Deep in his mind, he was expecting to find himself in a pit of deadly, exotic snakes; hungry and full of venom, launching their bodies at his ankles.

Something was wrong with the air; it felt thick and humid. The walls seemed as though they wanted to close in, crushing the life out of Kyle and Jack. And the idea of that was weighing on Kyle's chest. He was never one to enjoy enclosed areas, but his claustrophobia was not so bad as to send him in a screaming panic from the room like a child who fears clowns after watching *Stephen King's It*.

There was something down here.

In Kyle's mind, he knew. He couldn't explain it too well; it was too complex for him to realize. This whole week had resembled a bad nightmare. He had to kill. He had to survive. He couldn't understand why. He always thought that he'd be safe. And this was not the occasional walking into a convenience store that's being robbed. This went way beyond the realm of reality into another category that hadn't been named yet.

He almost envisioned it. It appeared to him like an underground church worshiping Evil, not praising God. It sat on an altar in the front, centered in a circle of tall, thick candles that burned brightly, almost fueled by Evil itself. It had an unusual marking on the cover; it looked worn and very old, something you'd find at a rare and used books store. The pages were crusted with age, stiff and creamed with faint yellowing around the edges. It was tainted with evil. It possessed unknown literature that Kyle knew had some great importance to his journey. It was like he was chosen; him, Jack, Rebecca; Kennedy, too—chosen for one reason or another. But why, he did not know. Things are rarely coincidental in life, Kyle had always thought. If it wasn't one thing, it'd be another, and another. There was no changing fate, only manipulating it, but the outcome would more than likely be the same: Death. It was the one thing in life that was guaranteed, sealed with a stamp from God. It was inevitable. The only unpredictability would be when and where. And as much as he kept it in the back of his mind, as much as he tried to concentrate on what stood before him; on Jack helping him, walking with him, Kyle thought that he was breathing some of his lasts breaths into the still air.

They could hear screaming in the far distance. Not just any kind of screaming, but a high-pitched moan like the sound that cats make when they're in heat in back alleys. Whatever it was, it didn't sound human. It sounded like a creature, or better yet a creature being tortured—or one that lusted for death and suffering. Kyle immediately thought that the monstrosity would be making a beeline down the endless passage way with nowhere to turn off, no nook to hide in; it was going to run straight for them, kill them, eat them, flay their skin right off their bones with swipes from its long, razor claws and its snapping needlepoint teeth. It would come. It would come and kill them all.

Jack didn't say a word. He kept calm and patient, reading his hand on his gun, focusing heavily on anything that might stand in front of him. The only person he trusted stood behind him. Kyle had been through a lot. Jack knew not to ask quite yet; he didn't want to be a cop right now and start questioning Kyle about his ordeal. His gold shield didn't matter where they were. He was a survivor. A man who had entered some place where normality didn't seem to exist, a place where nightmares were reality and reality was just a figment of some poor bastard's imagination.

It cried out again, wailing.

Chains rattled.

Walls shook.

It was coming.

* * *

Daniel found himself in rooms inside of rooms, much like a maze without the piece of cheese dangling at one end for a mouse's reward. He kept quiet, walking over the dead, passing by the walls of human ornaments—very few remained alive. It was all with the keeping. Like Daniel, this place had never known good intentions.

Daniel was an evil man, but you couldn't tell until his beady eyes stared at you, his face grimaced with hatred and rage and he'd shank you with any sharp metal object he could. He'd learned that in prison, which seemed like a lifetime ago. It had been nine years since he had gone into the California Prison System for a sacrificial murder. The judge had ruled fifty-five years without the possibility of parole until a man showed up confessing to the murder. He was a follower of Daniel's, an elderly man who gave up his life so that Daniel could continue on his journey, his quest for the truth and for the power that came with it.

Daniel had served seven months in prison, and in that time he had learned all sorts of tricks on makeshift weapons. He'd seen everything from melted toothbrushes with the end sharpened to a point to tape wrapped around a jagged rock for a handle. Prisoners can be very creative when they need to be. And though Daniel was the new guy in Prison Block B, no one bothered him; they knew not to, as if a stronger force than their urge to intimidate overcame their instinct.

Daniel had crossed the line from the regular world to this world. It was a world in between worlds. This was a world where ghosts visited, kindred spirits traveled the walls and walked the streets, not knowing where to go or how to get there.

Those volumes of books were the key to crossing over, to eliminating the medium and having two conjoining worlds where one race would rule all. Mankind versus the darkest enemy that they'd ever witnessed. Daniel would be the general of the Dark Army, and Necromancer would be ruler of all.

The air was thick and dank. The walls were made of concrete blocks and lit with torches all in a row. To his right lay a stairway leading downward. The concrete steps had no railings and were off balance; one misguided step and it could send you barreling over to your death.

Daniel saw the darkness. He listened.

He walked down the dimly lit steps, keeping his right hand on the wall for guidance. He followed the stairs down to the final level of the complex.

It led to a room that was unbelievable to his eyes. It looked like a church. The room had everything from a cathedral ceiling to stained glass windows. But the walls, the floor, and the pews were made of gold. Daniel had never seen anything like this before. The room was probably worth billions; just a tenth of a pew would send a seven-digit check your way. But money was of no consequence to Daniel. He wanted power, and sometimes the need for power outweighs the lust for wealth.

In the back of the church, he saw it.

It sat on its own pedestal surrounded by thick, white candles burning so brightly that it was almost hard to look directly at it.

The Book of Necromancer sat in the middle, its binding closed.

Daniel grinned wickedly like he had just hit the jackpot in Atlantic City. But to him he *had* hit the jackpot. This was his dream realized. He would finally have the power to call upon Him. He would now be able to control the army of the Dark Ones to rule once and for all.

"What do you think you're doing?" a man asked from behind.

"Who the fuck are you?" Daniel replied, reaching for his knife.

"You won't be needing that here," the man said. "And if you want to know my name, you must only ask."

"Well then who the fuck are you?" he demanded angrily.

"Miller," he told him. "I run this place, and I'm afraid this is off limits to you."

"The hell it is," Daniel taunted. "I came for that book, and I'm not leaving without it."

"I'm afraid you will have to."

"You planning on stopping me?"

"No."

"Good choice."

"He is." Miller pointed to the back of the church where black curtains were draped in the background concealing two exits on either side, but Daniel did not see the way out. He saw It instead.

It was tall and as black as night. It had a long snout, sharp claws, and some sort of self-contained goo dripping over itself, like slime or drool that was spewing from its pores. Its face was long and snarling; evil had stamped its mark and it was this animal.

"What the hell is that!" Daniel's voice cracked like a child hitting puberty.

"My pet," Miller said with the utmost confidence.

Daniel stared at it. He knew that if Miller gave the command, he wouldn't be able to run from it fast enough. It looked like a hybrid between dinosaur and man, but it was neither. It was a new breed, perhaps a demon that he had never come across in all of his books and studies, or perhaps it was man's creation. There were dozens of variables, none that Daniel wanted to think over. He wanted that book. He would die to get his hands on it; and die he might do.

"Listen, all I want is the book," Daniel said, almost pleading.

"But it does not belong to you."

"It doesn't belong to you!"

"Now, now," the man who called himself Miller said calmly, "no need to shout."

Daniel felt as though he was being patronized, and all he wanted to do was to run that blade through the guy's stomach and have it rip out his back, to feel the warm suckle of blood rinse off his hands, to smell that copper scent — but then the beast would surely come after him.

Daniel had the Dark Ones on his side. He could call upon them if he had that book. Soldiers would appear from thin air, obeying all of his commands, including attacking that animal that waited in the corner, drooling, growling like a '66 Ford Firebird's engine.

"Daniel," Miller said, "greed will get you nowhere."

"How do you know…"

From behind, the mutant opened its mouth and slammed it shut over Daniel's neck, tearing it clean off. Blood splattered the golden walls and floor and speckled Miller's face. Miller grabbed a white handkerchief from his pocket and wiped himself clean. He smiled as he watched Daniel's body fall to the ground, blood still pouring profusely from his open neck, his head lost in the gullet of the creature; bones crushing, skin tearing while it digested.

*Joseph McGee*

# XXIII

January 30th, 2009 8:34A.M.

Jack fell silent when he saw the graves.

They were unmarked like lost souls traveling through eternity. No one would ever know their names. God only knew how long they'd been there. Had they been just like Jack and Kyle, two normal people traveling to the Great Unknown, or had they been captured here like the men and woman who filled up the walls in a bloody heap, their bodies resting inside the walls like the catacombs in Vatican City, entombed underneath the earth?

It was like a rodent, racing its way to Jack with an open, hungry mouth. It was hairless and brown, with a forehead that was distinctly wrinkled. It eyes were orange, like burning embers; its claws long and clicking on the ground, like the sound of a horse's hooves.

Jack pointed the black eye of his gun barrel at it. He fired one shot, then a second. The brass shells leaped from the gun and jingled onto the ground.

It stopped moving and lay there, dead.

This was a godforsaken road traveling to the end of all they had come to know.

The path curved slightly to the right and led to another room; a larger, grander room with lit chandeliers and tables and chairs. Dinner had been served: Turkey with mashed potatoes and green beans, and beverages to the right of every plate. There must have been seating for fifty people.

Kyle searched the large room carefully, looking for any movement. Then he ran to the nearest table and drank what was in the brown wooden cup. Fortunately, it was water. Kyle had never tasted anything purer in his life. It quenched his thirst almost immediately, but it still wasn't enough. Kyle gulped down three cups of water in less than a minute, then ate someone's turkey. A leg, then a breast. It was baked with sweet spices of all sorts; it was delicious.

Jack was more cautious. He waited for Kyle to finish stuffing himself; turkey grease was smeared on his face and mashed potatoes were dabbed on his nose. Kyle used no fork or knife, just his bare hands, trying to juggle the turkey leg and the gun at the same time.

Jack joined him.

Kyle hadn't eaten in almost a week. He was acting like a homeless orphan child. He belched and laughed in such wicked pleasure that he had finally found something to eat, something to drink. At least he wasn't going to dehydrate or starve to death.

Jack joined him in a glass of water, but that was it. He allowed Kyle to finish eating while he stood lookout.

Kyle stopped eating in mid-chew. He noticed something about the table. Something was off—with the walls too. There was something strange about the paintings on the walls.

The pictures were of the same image, only differing slightly in size. They all portrayed a deep navy background with a man in a dark robe shrouding his face. You could only see his eyes as red as blood peering out through the darkness.

The tables were etched by some kind of wood-burning instrument, and portrayed the backside of the man in the paintings with that same dark robe that could only represent death. Kyle noticed how the artist had made the robe stand still, as if on a windless night; how it covered the man's identity perfectly.

One more puzzle needed to be solved; one more mystery to unravel.

Kyle pushed himself away from the table, looking all around him at the other similar tables that varied in size like the four paintings on the wall. He looked at them and it clicked in his head. And to himself he repeated: *Size. Portions. Alignment. Organization.* They were all good reasoning and resolution.

Jack looked up at him. "Are you okay?"

"There's one more thing we need to solve, and let's pray to God I'm right."

"What are you talking about?"

"The paintings, the tables—they need to be aligned," he explained.

He moved the first table over to the second spot, the second table to the first. The fourth went to the third, and the third went to the fourth. He had aligned them by size, from shortest to longest, which, if he'd done it correctly, led him to the painting on the left wall, the one Jack had been standing under.

Kyle pocketed the gun in his waistband and allowed power and fury and anger to wash over him like a baptism. He ran for the wall and leaped into the air, legs expanding into a crescent kick. Kyle connected with the wall and bricks shattered into stones and pebbles. He fell back, hitting his head on the hard cement floor. He was stunned for a moment, but then the adrenaline took over and he felt no pain.

The bricks were thin and hollow and would have come down with a good swift kick, without all the momentum and force from Kyle's running that seemed more like something Jet Li would do in one of his action movies.

Kyle climbed to his feet and shouted, "This way!"

Jack followed him, climbing over the rubble of stone and debris, covering his mouth from the cloud of dust. They headed into a dark and forbidden dwelling, a place that looked as though it had not seen the light of day in centuries.

Jack couldn't figure out why he had followed Kyle in here. He wanted to look for an escape, to go back up to where he had first lost sight of Rebecca and the police cars.

But it would have been fucking insane to leave Kyle all by himself to defend off some big bad-ass fucker. Jack had more of a heart than that. He had been a cop for years, been through shootouts and car chases and foot pursuits. And yet he wondered to himself why he'd been alive after all this time. It didn't take a rocket scientist to see that being a cop drops your livelihood rate at least by a few percent, and then doing all the crazy shit he'd done to catch the bastard just lowered the fucking thing more. So why in the hell was he here? Why was he so determined to help Kyle? He was a local cop. They had federal agencies for stuff the local P.D. couldn't handle, and that busted Jack's balls more than anything. He called them the Men in Black. Each time he'd see a Fed, he'd be wearing a nice suit: black sports coat, black tie, and black slacks with a white button-down shirt. Jack had yet to see one wearing an AC/DC t-shirt and blue jeans. That might be out of their dress code, the my-rectum-is-so-tight dress code.

Jack squeezed tightly on the butt of the gun, waving his hands around the darkened path that sloped and curved like a zigzag; Kyle was already a good ways ahead, trotting along like he had bat-vision and could see as clear as daylight breaking through.

"C'mon, Jack. Almost there," Kyle coaxed.

Jack was almost annoyed. He wasn't sure if it was because of Kyle arrogance and lack of self control or because he was younger and could do things that Jack couldn't anymore. Not to say that Jack was over the hill or anywhere near retirement; he had years left on the force, good years before he'd have to take a desk job answering calls and signing documents.

Kyle screamed in horror.

Jack, not quite knowing how far the scream was coming from, ran to his aid as fast as his legs would carry him, saying to himself *You should've fucking waited for me, kid.*

Jack saw it, too.

They were in the walls.

Bodies were pushing through the concrete like it was Jell-O; imprints of their hands and faces were coming through clearly, their mouths opened as if to speak to them, perhaps warn them before it was too late.

The walls were written on with the same type of picturesque drawings Kyle had seen earlier.

They were the same, except for a final piece that he knew wasn't there before.

The last picture showed a man who had killed a monster. The man was kneeling before the creature in honor of his victory while the dark monstrosity lay dead. And Kyle couldn't help but to think that he was that man—or was it Jack? Either way, it had a good outcome and that's the only thing Kyle wanted. He wanted to be safe again, to go home; he wanted to see Kennedy once more, to be able to talk about their lives together, to build a new one far away from Snow Hill, far away from all this fucking bullshit that he found himself way too deep in. He would take her away from here, maybe to North Carolina. He'd heard it was nice down there. It'd be a great place to start over again—if he made it out of here alive.

It called out to him.

Whispers in Kyle's head mumbled to him, like a muffled voice on the other end of a phone line. They frightened him. He was struggling to tune them out like turning the dial on a radio, but the same static kept humming.

Jack followed behind Kyle to where there was light. An archway of fire lined the walls where the dead came out of the cement and warned the weary travelers, trying to scare them off never to return again—or to ask them to follow the path to the ass-end of Hell itself.

Blood marked the walls at the end of the pathway.

Hell had been re-imagined.

The stains that spotted walls in slashes were fresh and still dripping. And through this wall another face appeared through the concrete, morphing the solid object around its body, almost as if it was trying to push through to free itself from the concrete prison in the nameless Hell that had entrapped its soul for eternity.

He stood in the room.

Jack would have recognized that pencil-necked prick anywhere. It was George Miller, president of the club.

He was in the back of a golden church with a large reptilian-like creature with large scales on its back, a face that resembled mythical dragons, and a tail that looked more like a whip with a spearhead at the end; Miller was petting it like a faithful Golden Retriever, scratching it underneath its chin and on its massive chest.

The walls, like many modern churches, had colored windows that told a picture of something, and the something was nothing like Jack ever heard about at Sunday School. The church was made out of a solid metal, resembling gold of the highest quality. The pews and the walls and the floors were the same. And a red carpet draped down the center of the aisle led to a golden altar. It was crafted into a monster, like a dragon but somehow different in many ways. Jewels that must have been rubies filled both eyes, emeralds made up its massive nostrils, and countless diamonds were used for the wide grin of deadly teeth. A book stood at a forty-five degree angle on top, clenched in a golden claw.

Jack prepared his gun.

Kyle stood at the entrance behind Jack, monitoring the surroundings. On the right, Kyle saw a dead carcass lying in a bloody mess, with limbs strewn about as if the man had been a rag doll being shaken about until all the stuffing came loose. And his certainly had; it spilled onto the golden floor.

Jack looked at Kyle, letting him know just by body language that he was going to stir up something here, that he'd make the first communication. Kyle nodded, giving him the go-ahead has he slowly pressed back on the hammer to his pistol.

"Something told me you were an asshole," Jack said, then echoed it a couple times over.

Miller turned around, surprised. He smiled. "Detective — you think you can take away my book?"

"Your book?" Jack asked, dumbfounded.

"Oh, don't be coy with me, sir. I know what you're after, just like that piece of shit over there."

Jack hadn't noticed the dead body before, or the smell stirring from his bowels and remains. "I'm not here for a book, jackass — I'm here to arrest you for a half-dozen murders," he told him. "That sounds better than reading a book to me, you sick fuck."

Jack walked toward Miller, slowly pacing himself down the red carpet between the pews. Kyle waited by the entranceway, ready to start a shootout with the bullets that remained; he was ready to use them all.

As Jack approached, the creature stood up to a full height of at least eight-feet tall, maybe nine. Its skin was unusually black with velvet dripping in some kind of bodily fluid.

Jack pointed the gun at the monster, eye level, squaring the barrel of the gun at its forehead.

"No need to use your weapon," Miller said. "Bullets won't hurt him." He walked over to the altar, leaving his pet by itself, almost growling, and grabbed the book. He turned around to face Jack and Kyle and raised his eyebrows as if he had repeatedly read from this book and was now getting annoyed from having to recite the same text over again. He spoke in a language that neither Jack nor Kyle had ever heard of before. It wasn't Spanish or Italian, French or German, but something different.

He recited words: Alkar maryantai tooblo sampsana moyank boytiquwe alessondrek.

Gusts of winds whirled around, spawning from nowhere.

In his mind, Jack said fuck it, and he opened fire on Miller, shooting him four times in the chest and a fifth time in his left eye socket which exploded the left portion of his head into small fragments of skin and bone. Miller fell to the ground and the book collapsed on top of him, closing shut. The creature trotted toward him, and a second one emerged from behind a long curtain that hung in the back, blocking any plausible escape route.

Jack opened fire until all of his rounds were spent.

Kyle fired his rounds, all but one shot making their marks in the second creature's head and chest. The final shot was off and ricocheted off a golden pew.

Kyle knew it was something about that book they were protecting, something that people had risked their lives to uncover. Kyle needed it, like the feeling of Kennedy's love in his heart. He raced to the right side of the church, passing the pews speedily, rushing over to the dead body, lifting the book from his chest, and clenching it under his arm like a football.

"Jack, I got it!" he said. "Let's get the fuck out."

Jack backed up to the entrance, allowing room for Kyle to run past him, then he followed.

This room was different. It wasn't the same one they had walked through before. The faces appearing through the morphed concrete had finished pressing through, and the walls were now made out of sheetrock and stitched together unprofessionally.

There was no means of escape, and now they were empty on ammo. Behind them, a thick and heavy concrete slab closed down, blocking off the reptilian creatures from ever setting foot in this cubical room.

Kyle opened the book. He could feel a power surge through him like nothing else had ever before. It electrified him—the air was now electrified. The book had writings that were hand-written in perfect penmanship, as if the author took his delicate time to write out everything with a perfect etiquette. But this book held more than just a story. Kyle read while Jack constantly asked him what he was reading, but Kyle had tuned him out for something much more important.

It was the story of Snow Hill.

The first entry in this logbook was dated centuries ago.

*The monster is something more than man and more demon. Thou killed many men. Thou called upon the darkness for help to kill men and women and children.*

*After our ship crossed the great ocean, we discovered something in the water. A monster, like the Bible had spoken about. It was Leviathan, the sea serpent with its many heads, casting people into a river of fire…*

While Kyle read the entries in the dusty journal, Jack used the butt of his gun to break through the sheetrock to the other side. It was as if the building was building upon itself, like it was alive and breathing its dark soul into the heart of all that was good and pure, just trying to survive in its natural habitat like creatures from different walks of life did.

Kyle flipped through the pages as if he were looking for a specific entry in a dictionary. He found drawings upon drawings of the same creature, all signed by different artists in fine print in one of the corners of the drawings, but with initials only: L.C.F., B.S.T., B.J.A., and K.A.L. were the only four artists in this book. It spoke of locating alternate doorways to something else, something further along than this world, a Hell that was once released on Earth.

The book came to life, swirling the text to nothing, then reappearing. Kyle dropped the book in surprise and backed away from it quickly.

He knew it was evil.

Then the screams began. Loud and echoing, moving closer like racing horses.

"Get us the fuck out of here!" Kyle yelled.

Jack didn't need for him to finish talking. He put his foot through the wall again and again and again, like a sledge hammer; he was using his foot so fiercely and meanly it was hurting him; blistering and bleeding, swelling. Jack finally broke through. He ushered Kyle through the small hole he had created. Clouds of white powder filtered through the air. They covered their mouths, trying not to breathe in anything that could be potentially hazardous.

Now it looked familiar: That path of bricks and ghostly faces appearing through the concrete, though they had stopped from pushing themselves through. This was the same place; Jack was almost sure of it.

Kyle ran back past Jack and grabbed the book. He thought that if people were willing to die to get their hands on this, it might make some sense of what the hell was happening all around them; the ghostly faces, the weird lights, the monstrosities at every turn, the wall of dead people with body parts sliced off. Some sense had to be made of it. Wind rustled in more strongly now, perhaps from some hidden room within the walls, or from cracks in the concrete foundation.

Now the book felt like skin, the kind of skin that has been out in the sun too long and acquired a deep sunburn.

It was alive.

It spoke to Kyle, filling his head with whispered memories and long-forgotten secrets, enlightening him with the past lives of time and the future of all existence. It was metamorphosing him, allowing him power no man had ever been given. He felt stronger, more alert, wiser. His eyesight had changed; he could focus much more clearly now and somehow zoom in to things like a pair of binoculars. His heart slowed to a steady beat and not the fast racket of a jackhammer pounding its way through cement.

In that touch, Kyle knew he had become a superior man amongst men.

Jack hurried Kyle along. They ran as the bricks deluged into dust and pebbles. The phantom bodies finally broke through. They screamed an angry moan as they rustled out of their dark tombs. They were skeletons not human faces.

Jack picked up speed, limping along as fast as he could with his injured foot.

"C'mon," he shouted, even though he was now the one trailing behind. They climbed up the staircase, racing against time and death.

At the top of the stairwell they waited for them. The dead bodies hung from the wall, naked with large piecing holes through their abdomens; men with their genitals hacked off, women with their breasts unevenly sliced from their bodies. Their eyes were white and ghostly, almost zombie-fied.

"What the fuck." Kyle barreled through like a defensive tackle; running, kicking, punching; swinging all around like a drunk in a barroom brawl trying to take on anyone he could.

Jack was close behind, hobbling his way along. Kyle reached for his arm and hustled him through.

The dead cried out like an echo inside a cave, each one sounding deeper than humanly possible. Some were on the ground covered in their own excrement; others were just pushed to the side by Kyle reaching back and finding the energy and the courage to break free of their grasps.

Kyle found himself where he started from.

The bedroom was the same; to the right was the crawl space where he and Chelsea had hid. She was dead, and he couldn't think about her anymore, at least not right now. But he would remember the beautiful young woman who had saved his life.

Kennedy was on his mind, flashing in still imagery in his head, and he smiled. He was going home.

He ran to the broken window, pulling Jack by the arm, hurrying him along before the dead could get the chance to move closer.

They jumped out.

Their bodies rolled into the cold snow mounds of a roof, much like a carport. They rolled until they fell off to a ten-foot drop. Kyle landed almost perfectly on his feet; Jack slapped the pavement with his back. He screeched in pain, his face grimacing in agony from the cracking of ribs.

"Jack, you okay?" Kyle rushed to his side. He waited a minute before trying to lift him up to his feet.

Kyle saw it first.

He saw the building. This was not the building he had entered. It was some translation of it. He looked around. The streets were lined with houses and cars and snow-covered trees that seemed ignoble in comparison to the ones he had known this street to have. It was all dark. The homes had fallen silent against the wind, like hollow graves.

And it began to snow something awful.

There was nothing noteworthy down the road, in either direction. No life at all. It was like the town had died. The once active city had been turned into a ghost town—or was this the Hell the book was talking about?

Kyle stood by Jack's side with the book under his arm, looking up, then left and right. He saw nothing but the falling flakes of white drifting down almost purposefully.

Jack could see the fear in Kyle's eyes; he could see the anguish pouring from his face, a sight that he too wore.

Kyle looked down at Jack, still holding his back, and said, "I just want to go home."

He sat down on the cold ground next to Jack, bringing him closer for warmth, and opened the book. Page one was dateless. Time had not begun.

And, like a sinner's prayer, he read on.

# ABOUT THE AUTHOR

Joseph McGee is the author of *In the Wake of the Night* and *The Reaper* among other titles. His short fiction has appeared in numerous magazines and anthologies like *The Sound of Horror, Help! and Shroud Magazine*. He's been featured as an Amazon.com bestseller with such titles as *Phil's Place, Darkness Won't Rest* and his three-story collection, *Tripartite,* which was featured in the Top 100 on Amazon.com Kindle titles.

He is a member of the Horror Writers Association and is a Board Member of the Southern Horror Writers Association; he is a Preditors & Editors award finalist.

Joseph McGee resides in Massachusetts and is a diehard fan of the 2008 NBA Champions, Boston Celtics.

Visit him at www.josephmcgee.net and check him out on MySpace! He replies to all of his messages personally.

Printed in the United States
125115LV00004B/1/P